The Mistletoe Mistake

SCARLETT KOL

The characters in this book are fictitious. Any similarity to real persons, living or dead, places, or events is coincidental and not intended by author.

*To those who love a sweet holiday romance
and don't care what others think about it.*

CHAPTER ONE

"To amazing friends and even better drinks."

I raised my shot glass and clinked it against Claire's matching one, already hoisted in the air. Bits of the sugar rim flaked off and drifted to the bar top like glittering flakes of snow.

"Here, here." Claire jerked her head back and downed the shooter with a cringe and a smile.

My stomach clenched. I'd never been able to handle shots. I'd had too many terrible nights that started with a few innocent drinks. But tonight would be different. Just one shooter. No more. Besides, after the last few days, I needed a little something to numb my brain. I licked the sweet sugared rim and took a deep breath. The liquor burned down my throat, but in a more pleasant minty way than the burn of straight tequila, or worse, whiskey. I wiped my mouth with the back of my hand as I forced myself to swallow.

Claire slammed her glass down on the bar. "Pretty good, huh? Another round?"

"Nope. I'm good." I put my glass beside hers and waved off Danny, the all-too-anxious bartender already waiting with a bottle of peppermint schnapps. "It tastes like I forgot to spit out my mouthwash."

"It's called Candy Cane Storm, what did you expect?"

"Of course it is." I swiveled on my stool and rested my back against the bar. Just another reminder of Christmas and how fast it kept creeping up, no matter how much I tried to deny it. I couldn't handle it this year. Everything was just too festive for my sour mood and nothing I did seemed to get me in the spirit. Why couldn't everyone skip it for one year?

I sighed at the lazy swoops of red and green lights strung around the room. They twined around the jukebox on the far wall as a melancholy version of "Have Yourself a Merry Little Christmas" drifted from its speakers. Bah humbug. I'd figured Danny's Tavern would be the safest place in Havenbrook to get away from all this obligatory celebrating, but for an Irish tavern, it held no luck. Just happy smiles and happier couples shining under the tacky holiday lights.

"It will be okay. It was a lousy month for this to happen, but at least now you know. He could have strung you along until January, and then you would've wasted all that time on the slime ball." Claire passed me a red cocktail in a hurricane glass and nudged her shoulder into mine.

"Thanks." I nudged her back and yanked out the

candy cane garnish, discretely sneaking it onto the bar behind me. "And at least I can return that camera I bought him. It cost a fortune."

"See, there is a bright side. Forget about Fletcher Hollingwood." She cast me a wary grin, then shifted on her barstool. "Besides, Holly Hollingwood completely sounds like a fake name. You dodged a bullet, my friend."

"Maybe." I laughed. Hearing her say it sounded odd now, but there had been so many times I'd dreamed about it being true. I'd pictured the white dress and the cake, and, until last week, I expected to see a ring under the tree this year. The way Fletch had been acting shifty around me lately. The calls from the jewelry store he tried to hide from me. Never once did I think it might be because he'd moved on with the girl who worked there. Dierdre. Ugh. Even the way it rolled off my tongue seemed wrong, dirty even. "But it's not just that. It's all this." I waved my arm in the air, trying not to upend my drink on my dress.

"Danny's. What's wrong with it? We come here all the time."

"No, it's the happy Christmas stuff. It's everywhere. I can't get away from it. Even at work, all I get are letters from people trying to make their Christmas romance come true. All those card companies and the movie industry have told everyone that you have to have the perfect Christmas. It's always 'Dear Holly, how can I make my next-door neighbor notice me' 'Dear Holly, I want to tell the woman on my bowling team that I love her during the holidays, what is the perfect present?' 'Dear Holly, how can I make sure I have the most magical holiday if my boyfriend doesn't celebrate Christmas?' It's exhausting."

Claire scanned me over as she sipped her drink. Her eyes narrowed, processing like a supercomputer. "Really? Because if I remember correctly, you told me you loved giving relationship advice. That it gave you purpose or some higher calling or whatever."

"I think I used to. But..." I tried to come up with a better excuse, but what was the point? Claire had stuck with me since high school and lying to her, let alone getting away with it, would be next to impossible. "How are people going to react when they find out I'm a fraud? If I can't keep a relationship together, how am I supposed to give them advice on what to do in their lives?"

She shook her head and laughed. "Are you kidding me? You're awesome at your job. Fletcher being a cheating loser isn't on you, honey. Besides, you've been doing this for over, what, three years now? People trust you, they aren't going to quit because of this."

I took a sip and squirmed on my stool, the cocktail pleasantly much fruitier than the awful shooter.

"That's not all, is it?" She leaned back against the bar, swirling her straw in her drink as she scrutinized my lousy posture.

I pushed my shoulders back and sat up. "What about your trip to Huatulco for New Year's? You and

Austin must be getting pretty excited. Only a few more weeks, then nothing but beaches, sun—"

"Nice try, Holls. You've always sucked at deflection, so just spill it."

"Alright. I'm tired of being 'Ask Holly' all the time," I said, with a loud sigh. "When I started this job, Jenkins promised it would only be temporary until a reporting job opened up and then I could work on being a proper journalist. Build my portfolio and move on to something bigger. But there have been five people who've been promoted to reporter jobs and I never get my chance."

"Have you asked though?"

"Every time. Jenkins just tells me I'm so good at my job and if I could hang on for a little while longer they will find the right person to fill my column and any position I want is mine. He keeps telling me that the corporation who owns the paper doesn't want to mess with what's working."

"Then tell him. Tomorrow morning, march into the office of Mr. Peter Jenkins III and tell him you're done putting up with his corporate mandate." She shook a defiant fist in the air, the momentum nearly knocking her off her stool. She straightened herself. "And if he doesn't give you a timeline on a reporter job, you're quitting."

"Quitting?" I choked. I loved the paper. I didn't want to quit.

"Of course, what else do you have to lose? You said you wanted to move on to bigger and better things.

Fletcher isn't keeping you in this town anymore. It's time to get what you want."

The seeds of regret washed away with Claire's encouragement. I'd come back to Havenbrook only to sit on the advice column for way too long. My college friends had bylines in major papers. They did the nightly news updates in towns much bigger than here. But I gave that all up so long ago, I couldn't possibly go back. Besides, I couldn't leave my home again. Could I?

"But what about you, Claire? I couldn't leave you."

"Of course, you could. We went to schools across the country and still found our way back to each other. Moving onward and upward is not going to change that. Besides, it would give me a place to go when my mother-in-law decides to come visit."

I slid from my stool and wrapped my arms around her. "You're the best, you know that?"

"Oh, I know." She patted me on the back, her soft auburn curls tickling my nose. "Just don't forget about me when you're super famous."

I laughed as the strains of Elvis' "Blue Christmas" whined through the air. "I don't think I'm quite done with Havenbrook yet, but I've had enough of this. How about some vintage Bon Jovi or something?"

"'Please Come Home for Christmas'?" She clamped her lips around her straw and winked.

Shaking my head, I turned away and shimmied through the bodies toward the far side of the bar. A typical Sunday night. Not enough time before the magic of the weekend ended to venture just over the border to a Kansas City pub, so Danny's packed up tight from dinner to closing time. The air seemed heavier the farther I strayed from the safety of the bar into the crowd. Loud, sweaty patrons filled every available space and pulled extra chairs to overfilled tables making it nearly impossible to pass. I held my drink over my head, regretting that I hadn't left it with Claire, but still in the habit of carrying it from clubbing in college.

Finally, I reached the electronic jukebox. They replaced the classic one a few years ago, and a pang of nostalgia stung in my chest. Why did everything need to change? Couldn't people appreciate the comfort in the familiar?

I flipped through the menus, trying to find anything that wouldn't make me want to rip my ears off, but the jukebox had clearly been programmed to force Christmas cheer down everyone's throats, like it or not. Near the end, I found a tolerable mid-90's throwback album, and clicked every track to keep the place holiday free until at least closing time, even though I'd already be long gone.

The guitar riff whined from the speakers and I inhaled deeply, my shoulders finally relaxing. I closed my eyes for a moment, letting the gritty rock music ease my mind. I whirled around.

Smack!

A wall of muscle slammed into me. My glass wedged between us as the colorful cocktail poured down the front of my dress before smashing into shards on the floor.

I jumped back from the mess and rammed my hip into the side of the jukebox. *Ow!* "What the hell?"

"I'm so, so sorry." Hands waved in front of me as I retreated from my assailant.

"Watch where you're going next time." I swiped the liquid from my outfit. The red coloring bled through the blue fabric and grew wider. *Great. My favorite dress, ruined.* Another thing I lost this month that I couldn't replace. Did the universe hate me that much?

"Of course, my apologies."

As I clenched my fists, I tried to swallow the dictionary of curse words forming in my mouth, but they came too fast. "Well, if you—"

I glanced up and locked eyes with the stranger. His sorrowful gaze pinned my insults to my tongue. Wide and bright, like old copper pennies worn over the years. A little damaged and dirty, but teeming with stories to tell.

"I really am sorry, miss. It's a little crowded in here and I…" He reached toward me but stopped before making contact. Instead, he slipped his hand into his pocket and pulled out a slim leather wallet with a faint monogram on the side. He slid a couple of hundred-dollar bills from inside and held them out in his long fingers. "Here, let me pay for the drink and the dress. I insist."

"Don't worry about it. It's just my luck, anyway." I shook my head, but he didn't waver. I could take it. After all, this was his fault. Besides, the money probably meant nothing to him. The way his navy suit jacket tapered on his broad shoulders screamed tailor-made and, even though he'd tried to dress it down with jeans, they fit too perfect not to be high-end designer. He pulled the look off, but it tried way too hard for this town. I'd bet he wasn't from anywhere close to here and I'd likely never see him again. Except, it wouldn't be too bad if I did. I could get used to seeing that handsome face at the grocery store every once in a while.

"I feel terrible," he said, pushing the bills closer.

"Well, that's apology enough. If you'll excuse me, I need to take care of this mess."

He cast his stare to the floor, finally setting me free, as he slipped the bills back into his fancy wallet. I stuck close to the walls and slipped my way through the bar to the ladies' room at the back. After wadding up a handful of wet paper towels, I scrubbed at my skirt, but the stain didn't fade. Maybe I should go ask him for the money. I'd spent way too much on this dress the first time, and I was definitely in the mood to replace it with another for some retail therapy.

One of the bathroom stalls swung open and Nancy from the coffee shop near the park cast me a sweet smile. Her eyes caught on the stain and she cringed with pity, or maybe just embarrassment for me. I grinned back as I tried to keep tears from welling and watched until the door closed behind her. I collapsed against the dingy bathroom wall, the cold stone seeping through my thin disaster of a dress. A few wet lines tickled down my face. Maybe Claire was right. I should quit and start over somewhere else. Somewhere no one knew who I was. Maybe somewhere that didn't have Christmas.

My phone vibrated in my pocket. A few drops of red had splashed across the screen, but no major damage.

Claire: Where did you go? Are you okay?
Me: I'm fine. Just need a minute.

I wiped my face and held onto the porcelain sink for a couple seconds, letting my heart rate go back to normal. Glancing in the mirror, I tried to will away the lines starting to circle in my puffy eyes. Red swirling through green—even my own corneas had turned festive. Ugh. I forced a plastic smile. At least until I could get home and close the door on everyone else, then cry myself to sleep like I'd done all week. I'd hoped tonight would be the first good day in a while, but no.

As the door opened, the babble of the bar hit me in the gut. Enough for tonight. Time to go home. I slipped along the short hallway into the main room as a familiar bouncy head of chestnut waves sashayed past me. The synthetic scent of cheap perfume. The scent I remembered when I looked at engagement rings Fletcher would never buy me. Dierdre. Yes, definitely time to go.

I picked up my pace and glared back, checking that she didn't see me. She disappeared through the bathroom door and I exhaled again. Too close.

"Holly, I didn't know you would be here tonight."

The relief evaporated and my stomach twisted as a familiar deep voice cut through the din.

"Why would you, Fletcher? My schedule is no longer your concern."

I crossed my arms, bracing myself and putting as much distance between us as I could. He looked good. Too good. Ash blond hair stylishly slicked back, instead of flopping in his eyes. A new outfit that didn't look like he'd left it on the floor last night. Polished. Like he used to when we first got together. But it would fade, and maybe this time he'd be the one ending up with a broken heart.

"You don't need to be so rude. I understand you're mad, but—"

"But nothing. You're lucky I'm being this polite." I raised my voice. "You cheated on me. For months."

He slipped his hand over his coiffed hair and looked back over his shoulder. Only a few people seemed to hear, and he smiled back at them with a courteous wave. Coward.

"Calm down, alright. Can't we just be civil about this? It's a small town and we both have our reputations to uphold."

"What, like, first class asshole?"

I shifted right, but he stepped in front of me. I tried going left, but he blocked that way too.

"Holly." He hooked his fingers around my wrist. "Can I just talk to you?"

I yanked my arm away and held it to my chest as I scowled back at him. "No."

Over his shoulder, something red caught my eye.

The handsome stranger stood swinging a holiday cocktail in the air trying to grab my attention. His stare narrowed on the back of Fletcher's head, then shot toward me. I looked away hoping to hide my shame.

A breeze whisked past, my hair blowing over my shoulder.

Dierdre slid beside Fletcher. She looked at me and her mouth fell open for a moment before she quickly recovered. "Oh, hi. It's Hailee, right?"

"It's Holly," I grumbled. "And you know that. Everyone knows everyone around here."

"Oops, sorry." She giggled and settled closer to Fletcher, clasping her hand in his. The gaudy Christmas lights glinted off her ring finger. My stomach hollowed. A gut punch so forceful I struggled to stand. Fletcher had been ring shopping, just not for me. *Well played, Dierdre.*

The bar began to spin as this awful night kept getting worse. "I…"

"There you are, I started to think you weren't coming back." The navy suit jacket and jeans appeared by my side, handing me the cocktail. He turned toward Fletcher. "Ladies. Always keep you waiting, am I right? But this one is totally worth it."

The stranger nuzzled his nose in my hair as he stealthily slid his mouth near my ear. He whispered, "I can leave, but it looked like you might need a hand. Nod if you want me to stay."

Fletcher's clenched jaw cut sharp ridges in his cheeks as his glare swung from the stranger to me and back again. Dierdre squirmed beside him and wrenched her hand out of his grip, flexing her suddenly scarlet fingers.

"Oh, you, always so sweet." I nodded and tapped my open palm on the stranger's taut chest. Clearly, he took care of himself. Nice. Very nice.

He tugged my arm and I stumbled closer into him. Fletcher's cheeks erupted, brighter than the artificially colored drink in my hand.

"I'm sorry, I don't believe we've met." The stranger stuck his hand out to Fletch. "I'm Ben."

He accepted the pleasantry, his arm pumping hard in some arrogant show of prowess, but Ben matched him shake for shake.

Fletcher's lips turned up into a sneer as something sinister flashed through his stare. "How long have you known Holly, exactly?"

"Well…" Ben gazed down at me. "Since…"

"Since college," I blurted. "Yeah, we knew each other in college and recently reconnected. Such great timing that we were both single again at the right time."

"Oh. That's convenient since Holly's never mentioned you before," Fletcher said.

Ben's arm tensed around my back, but he regrouped and tilted forward toward Fletcher. "I doubt she would. I've always been crazy about her, but I didn't think she ever even noticed me back then. Whoever let her get away was an idiot, but their mistake was my good fortune."

Ben flashed Fletcher a refined smile. Perfect teeth

peeked through his dark red lips. Why he defended me, who knew, but the pained look on Fletcher's face was worth more than the crisp bills in his wallet.

I took a sip of my drink to clear the lump growing in my throat and to, hopefully, get another hit of courage. "And just in time for the holidays too. It must be fate."

He turned his flawless smile toward me. "Absolutely. My Christmas Holly hanging out under the mistletoe."

I dropped my head back. The gaudy plastic green and white mistletoe hung above us in a nest of metallic silver garland.

Fletcher folded his arms as his smug, twisted smirk returned. "Sounds like we aren't talking about the same person. Holly isn't that kind of girl."

My blood boiled. His hurtful words, the alcohol, and the embarrassment blended in a dangerous combination. Without thinking, I raised up on my tiptoes and planted my lips on Ben's. His eyes widened and he froze under my touch.

Oh no. Oh no. What did I just do?

But he didn't pull away. His hand fell to the small of my back and tugged me closer as his lips moved against mine. Slow, but determined. Powerful. Fletcher wasn't wrong. I wasn't the kind of girl who made out in public, especially with mysterious strangers whose names I barely knew. But where had that gotten me? And now as Ben's arms encircled my waist, I couldn't come up with a reason I'd held back so long.

I slid my free hand to his cheek and he responded, taking more of my mouth as his slight patch of tasteful stubble scratched against my chin. The sweet sting of bourbon grazed the tip of my tongue as I drifted deeper into him. Away from this bar. Away from Fletcher.

Movement flashed beside us and I snapped back into the present. Dierdre spun around and disappeared into the crowd. Fletcher scowled, then tossed a hand in the air before chasing after her.

Ben's lips relaxed and he rested his forehead against mine. He chuckled, his warm breath stoking the fire smoldering in my chest. "Nice to meet you too, Holly."

CHAPTER TWO

*M*y hands slipped into Ben's silky chocolate locks and held tight to the back of his head as his kisses trailed down my neck. Tingles shot through my entire body and conjured thoughts I shouldn't have. I didn't even know him, but I didn't care. Lips, tongues, and teeth all whirled together in a tornado of sensation. So much better than Fletcher. So much better than any other guy I'd ever met. My hand met his face again, my palm burning hotter and hotter against his skin. The rest of my body blazed. I...

"Earth to Holly. Come in, Holly."

Claire's voice cut through the fog as her hand waved in front of my glazed stare.

"Wait, what?"

The harsh lights of Corner Brew flicked on and I slammed my paper coffee cup onto the wood-grained countertop. I blew against my palm, attempting to cool the growing patch of sizzling skin, scalded from my mocha latte.

Claire laughed and retrieved a cardboard jacket from the front counter, then slipped it over my cup. "That's why you need to start bringing your own mug. Way fewer injuries."

I rubbed my eyes and picked up the cup with my uninjured hand. "Yeah, right."

"Jeez. What's with you this morning? Do you seriously have a hangover? We only had a few drinks with that Ben guy, I didn't think you'd had that much."

"No." I scowled at her, but she simply rolled her eyes and poured a generous helping of milk into her green plaid tumbler. "I didn't sleep well."

"No kidding. You look like hell."

"Uh ... thanks?"

"You're welcome." She nodded and smoothed my hair over my ear, taming the stray strands that always shot straight up from my crown. "But seriously, this is supposed to be your big day. The day you stand up for what you deserve. I'd think you'd want to be on the top of your game."

I glanced at my reflection in the coffee shop window. She wasn't wrong. Bags drooped under my eyes and I hadn't even tried to cover them with makeup this morning. My eyeliner swooped in crooked lines and forget even trying lipstick today. I swept my caramel strands back and secured them with an elastic at the nape of my neck. Better, but not sophisticated like Claire. Her bright eyes, rosy cheeks, and sleek bun taunted me in the glass door as we pushed our way out into the street.

"Maybe I should wait to talk to Jenkins? I'm really not in the right state to do this now. I could always do it tomorrow."

Claire linked her arm with mine. "Oh no, I'm not letting you chicken out. Do you want to be a real reporter?"

"Of course, I do."

"Then get over yourself and ask for what you deserve. Confidence is a very attractive quality, Holls. You'll be fine."

"Maybe I'm not that confident."

My feet nearly slipped out from under me as Claire crashed to a halt without letting go of my arm. "Are you kidding me? Where is the girl who was kissing hot strangers at the bar last night?"

My cheeks flamed. The fluffy snowflakes drifting through the sky landed and melted on my skin. "You mean the girl who kissed one hot stranger, chatted him up, then awkwardly left without her jacket or purse?"

"It wasn't that bad. Besides, I totally didn't mind walking the four blocks in the snow to your house to return your things when I have back-to-back client meetings today." She grinned as her sarcasm hit its mark and stung between my eyes.

"I'm so sorry, Claire." I dropped my head on her shoulder. "I think I just got flustered. I don't know what it was about that guy, but I'm totally embarrassed."

She squeezed my arm and tugged me closer. "Like you already said, you have no idea who he is and you'll probably never see him again, so who cares? Besides, the look on Fletcher's face when he stormed out of there with Dierdre was one hundred and ten percent worth it."

"Really?" I perked up and pictured the delicious image in my head.

"Oh yeah. He's probably off licking his wounds somewhere right now."

"He totally deserves it," I said.

"Yep. He totally does. In fact, he deserves so much worse than that. If Austin ever—"

"Don't even say it. He would never. You guys are perfect for each other." I held my cup up in the air until Claire clinked her travel mug against it. "Besides, he knows he'd have to deal with me if he did and that wouldn't be pretty."

"Speaking of not pretty, we're finally going to do something about those awful honey oak kitchen cabinets over the holidays. Renovating the whole room actually. You should see my inspiration pictures." Claire held out her phone and clicked the power button on. "Shoot. It's later than I thought. I'll have to show you another time."

Claire tucked her phone back in her pocket and shuffled across the sidewalk toward the revolving door of the First Street Bank. "Now remember, eye contact, stick to the facts, and don't take no for an answer. Got it?"

"Yes, boss."

She winked and wagged her index finger at me. "And don't forget to text me when it's over. I want to hear all about your success."

"Bye, Claire."

She disappeared into the bank, off to save the world again, one checking account at a time. I let out a deep breath and watched the hazy steam circle around my head in the winter chill. I could do this. I'd asked Jenkins so many times before, but this one felt so final. The Havenbrook Herald meant everything to me. My life. If I couldn't make this work, I didn't have a clue what I'd do next. But it didn't matter, Jenkins was going to give me that position and I'd have a long, happy career here. I leaned against the building and took a sip of my latte as the rough stone bricks teased hair out of my haphazard ponytail. I closed my eyes and faced the sky, letting the snowflakes cool me down and, hopefully, calm my nerves. *That's it. I could do this.*

The image of Ben's delicious mouth on mine flashed through my memory. His hands on my skin. I snapped my eyes open again and pressed a finger to my lips. Like I could still feel him there. I groaned and took another sip of coffee. How was I going to focus enough to ask for a promotion when I couldn't get that kiss, or that guy, out of my head?

"Morning, Holly. How was your weekend?" Doris chirped when I walked in and it lifted the clouds over my tense mood a little. Twenty years as the receptionist at *The Herald* and never a complaint. Just a bright grin to greet people and a kind heart to back it up. She'd been the first person I met when I'd come here as a kid. And she'd sat with her encouraging smile as I pushed open that door, as a nervous rookie hoping for her hometown editor to give her a chance. Doris gave me the friendly push I needed to get through the interview that day. Maybe she'd be my good luck charm again?

"Uneventful." *If you didn't count last night.* "How are you doing?"

"Oh busy, busy as always. Getting gifts wrapped for the grandkids. I can't wait to see their darling little faces on Christmas morning." Her face beamed with pure delight, her short gray locks crowning her head like a halo. I almost felt bad about cringing when she mentioned Christmas, but it wasn't her fault I'd suddenly become a cynic.

"Sounds wonderful. Do you know if Jenkins, I mean Peter, is in the office yet?"

"Yes, he was in before I was this morning, but he left a note that he'd be in solid meetings until ten and not to disturb him." She adjusted her glasses on her nose and looked over a yellow post-it note with Jenkin's scrawl across the surface.

Strange. Peter Jenkins typically waltzed into the office right before the nine am pitch meeting without even a second to take off his coat. "Great thanks. Any chance you can squeeze me in at ten o'clock?"

She glanced at her computer screen and clicked around a few seconds. "You bet. All scheduled."

"Perfect. Thank you."

I pushed through the door into the office and settled into my typical dingy blue cubicle. Except today, a bushy strand of cheap plastic holly circled my space. Cute. Really. Whoever did this needed to be crossed off the nice list. I pulled it off the fabric walls and re-pinned it on the outside of my cube so I didn't have to look at it. Managing my own column meant that I typically didn't work in the office as long as I made it to the pitch meeting and met my deadlines, but it also meant the short lot on desk selection. Even Coby the intern's desk met the minimum requirements to be considered bigger than a closet.

After finishing the last of my latte, I fired up my laptop and sat back as the OS icons spun on the screen. I reached into the bottom drawer of my desk and pulled out a thick manila file folder. Some articles were from college, clipped from the campus paper. Others I'd written every time I thought I had a chance at a reporter spot. Every time I'd been let down. I flipped through a more recent one on the top about the union negotiations at the meat packing plant last fall. It was good. Tight prose. Good grammar. Eyewitness accounts. But it didn't matter. Jenkins wouldn't even look at them, he'd just sigh and run his wrinkled hand over his chin before he assured me that my day would come and I needed to be patient. But I couldn't wait any longer. Electricity sparked in my veins and prickled against my skin. Something had to change.

"Hey there, 'Ask Holly'."

I cringed at the nickname and spun around in my chair, as I closed the file folder, dropping in back into the bottom drawer.

"Morning, Jesse."

He leaned against the small entrance to my cube, the unsteady walls tilting and threatening to fall. He'd been here a few months less than me, moving from a stint in Chicago as a crime reporter, back to his hometown of Havenbrook and away from the buzz of the city. Also taking another reporter job I'd never get. But at least I couldn't argue with his credentials and he always went out of his way to be benevolent. Jealousy didn't stand a chance against his positive attitude.

"Have you heard that Jenkins is making a big announcement this morning?"

"No. I haven't heard anything. What's it about?"

Jesse shrugged, the kind lines around his eyes wrinkling. "Not a clue. My daughters did some baking this weekend, so I went by his house to drop off some cookies and his wife said he'd received a call from corporate on Friday night and spent the entire weekend in the office. I stopped by on Sunday to bring in a piece for the holiday issue and sure enough, the door of his office was closed but the lights were definitely on."

"Strange. Hopefully, it's nothing serious. Maybe he's retiring or something?" Which could be perfect. If I could convince him to put me in a reporting spot, the next editor would have to deal with that decision.

"Well, let's get going, I doubt we are going to want to miss this."

I snatched a notebook and pen from my bag, then raced down the hallway after Jesse. The board room had already started to fill, but Jenkins hadn't arrived yet. I took my usual spot at the far end of the table, next to the window, and positioned my notes in front of me. Then a lump of dread collapsed in my stomach.

"Shoot, Jesse. Save my seat, I forgot something at my desk."

As I rushed back through the office, I popped up on my tiptoes to see if Jenkins left yet, but his door remained closed. *Perfect.* I grabbed the folder from the drawer and quickly typed my password into my laptop. My latest article for my non-existent job appeared on the screen. I hit print. I couldn't risk going in with a dated piece. This one about the community center embezzling scandal would be sure to grab headlines. I sprinted to the printer on the far side of the room and stuffed the still-warm pages into my folder.

The board room door clicked closed across the office. Late. Not a good impression to make when you're about to ask for a promotion. I bolted past the cubicles and paused at the door to catch my breath. After swiping my hair back and straightening my skirt, I rapped my knuckles on the door and slowly crept in.

Jenkins stood at the end of the table and waved me in. "And this is our fantastic advice columnist, Holly Brighton of *Ask Holly.*"

He rambled on about my accomplishments and my cheeks scorched. Normally, the attention would be enough to cause the blush, but I hadn't even heard Jenkins' words. Beside him, in an impeccable pinstripe suit and solid black tie, stood the stranger from the bar. His lucky penny eyes exploded as he caught my gaze.

"And Holly, please meet Benjamin Concorde from Concorde Publications Media. He's here to take *The Herald* digital."

CHAPTER THREE

ait, what? Digital? The *Havenbrook Herald* was an institution in this town. It predated the majority of print publications in the area. But the even bigger question? Out of the thousands of people who worked for head office, why did they have to send Ben?

Jesse pushed my chair back from the table and I dropped into my seat, as the folder made a loud smack on the table. I glanced down at my lap, wishing I could hide in my pocket until after the new year. And a Concorde? No wonder he had no issue shelling out hundreds like Halloween candy, his family owned half the papers on the East Coast, and the ones they didn't own outright they had a considerable share in them.

"I know this will be a difficult transition for everyone, but advertising revenues are down across the country and we need to keep up with the times. We've converted papers in St. Louis, Charleston, D.C., and

Detroit with amazing success and we'd like to continue that model with some of the smaller regional outlets."

I dared to look up. Ben stood with his hands in his pockets, trying to look comfortable and failing miserably. His slicked-back hair screamed of skyscrapers and working lunches, not small towns and their salt of the earth mentality.

"Excuse me." I raised my hand as I scanned the shocked and withering faces of my colleagues.

"Yes, Ms. Brighton, is it?"

His stare locked on my face and weighed heavy on my neck. A glimmer of a grin curled across his lips as he said my name. The lips that not even twelve hours ago were smashed against mine in the back of a pub.

"Are you sure this is the right move for Havenbrook? All those urban centers sound wonderful, but things move differently here. People are different around here. They still rely on a physical paper. Half the seniors in this town don't even own an electronic device."

He smirked as he watched me. The rest of the room seemed to fall away and I shook my head to break the eerie spell.

"Then they will need to get with the times, I guess. It's not feasible for this outlet to keep bleeding revenues with little hope of recovering them. I hear what you're saying, but sometimes change is a good thing."

"And sometimes change can kill a good thing," I added.

Ben jerked his head to the side, his brow furrowing as he glanced over at Jenkins.

I slapped my hand over my mouth. I'd crossed a line, and it didn't seem like anyone else planned on speaking up.

Jenkins shot me a stern glare. "Mr. Concorde will be meeting with each of you individually this week to go over the plan and to make a feasible route forward regarding the future of *The Herald*. I'm sure he would be willing to hear your concerns at that time."

"Of course, Peter," I said, then leaned back in my chair.

Ben nodded, his confident grin disappearing into the stuffy office air. "I know this might be a tough transition for some of you and there will be some changes coming." He glared at me and I focused on my pen, refusing to give him the satisfaction of knowing that he'd hit his mark. "But I assure you that I want to make it as easy as possible for everyone involved and ensure things go smoothly for our January 1st rollout."

Less than three weeks. How did he think he was going to make a change this dramatic in that little time? Especially with the holiday issue coming out so soon. Completely ludicrous.

Jesse shifted uneasily in his chair along with half of the other staff. I got it. I really did. Magazines went digital ages ago, but this wasn't Cosmopolitan or Vogue. This was *The Herald*.

"Watch for meeting invitations from me in the

next couple of days. I look forward to hearing what everyone has to say."

Do you, Ben? Do you really, or is that what you've been trained to spew to the low-life peons who prop up your family's money? Whoa. I blinked and tried to clear my head. The cocktail of emotions surging through my head better get back in line or I was going to make a fool out of myself in front of this guy. Again.

Jenkins stepped in front of Ben, hiding him away like a puppet at the end of a show. "That's all for today. I know everyone is working on the holiday issue so we'll save pitches until later, but if you have anything in particular you need to address, come to me directly. Thank you all for your time."

Jesse shook his head and a low whistle escaped his lips. I pushed away from the table and collected my things, trying to get out of this stifling room as quick as possible.

"And Holly," Jenkins called, still standing at the front of the room. "I can meet now unless you'd like to wait right until ten for our meeting."

I glanced down at the file folder in my hand and my shoulders drooped. "Never mind, Peter. It sounds like you have more important things on your mind right now."

We retreated to our cubicles, wordless and sloth-like. Zombies. I grabbed my phone and texted Claire.

Me: Not going to happen today. Long story. Talk later.

I didn't wait for a response, just chucked the phone back into my coat pocket and closed my laptop. If I wasn't going to be talking to Jenkins, there wasn't any reason for me to be here. I could go through my email and write my column at home. Besides, my stomach suddenly ached. I slid open the bottom desk drawer and flipped through the folder one last time. The ache deepened, spreading through my chest. Or maybe it was only my heart breaking again? It was so damaged now I doubted I would know.

"So, you're a journalist."

I jumped and the folder slipped from my hand. My articles flew through the air and scattered across the beige carpet and a pair of stylish black dress shoes.

"Are you determined to make me drop everything I touch?" I stooped down and scrambled to collect the pages, chucking them haphazardly into the drawer.

Ben crouched. "I'm sorry. I didn't mean to startle you." He picked up the last article, the one I'd just printed and hoped to present to Jenkins, even though that was never going to happen now. He skimmed the first few sentences. "I thought you were the advice columnist. Peter didn't mention that you wrote headline too."

"I don't." I snatched the pages from his grip and shoved them in the drawer, then closed it with a metallic thunk. "I'm just 'Ask Holly'. That's it."

"Well, that story looked pretty good. Needs a decent polish, but a great start."

A great start? Fantastic. No wonder I hadn't been

able to convince Jenkins to give me more responsibility.

"Not that it matters now. Once we go digital, we'll start cutting back on staff, start bringing in articles from Reuters and other presses until there's nothing left," I said.

Ben frowned and pushed back to standing with an effortless roll. "What makes you say that?"

"Because it happens all the time."

I followed his lead and stood, straight as possible to narrow the few inches he towered over me. Working in a predominantly male office wasn't always easy, but I'd held my own. I'd been a wreck lately, but no way would one outsider knock me back down. Even if his smoldering stare made my knees shake and I couldn't forget the feel of those soft lips— which could utter my career death sentence at any moment. "I may not be as connected as you are, Mr. Concorde, but I can assure you, I have contacts at other publications. I know what the collateral damage of a restructure like this looks like. Pardon me, if I'm a little sensitive about it when my job could be on the chopping block."

He tensed at the accusation and stepped back. "That's fair. There will probably be some cuts, but I'm hoping to minimize that as much as I can. Maybe you could help me since you seem so passionate about the project? I could use someone who knows *The Herald* but has also seen some of the world past the county line. Sound like a workable plan?"

Ben extended his hand, and I stared at it. Sell my

soul for a potential stay of execution? Maybe. But considering his only opinion of me was the train wreck of a girl who kissed people she didn't even know, I needed to make a better impression.

"Alright, Mr. Concorde. We have a deal." I shook his hand with my sturdiest grip. He raised an eyebrow as he studied me. Maybe I'd already made a statement. "Now if you could please excuse me, I have work to do."

CHAPTER FOUR

Dear Holly,

I'm trying to plan an unforgettable Christmas for my girl-friend, but I...

  I pinched the bridge of my nose and groaned, trying to inhale the scent of Mrs. Baker's blueberry pie to calm my nerves. Another Christmas romance letter. There seemed to be more and more of them every year. Didn't ... *what was his name again?* ... Smitten by the Season, know that he was cutting it a little too close to ask for my advice now and still plan on pulling anything off in time? Or that he could've simply read any of my articles from the past two months to glean ideas from? Articles I'd painstakingly written while trying to push down my nausea. But at least it would be a few weeks reprieve before the Valentine's requests started coming in. Assuming I still had a newspaper to write for by then.

As if sensing my uncomfortable tenseness, the tiny bell over the diner door chimed and Benjamin Concorde blew in on the winter wind, a trail of snowflakes following behind and dotting the checkered linoleum floor. He brushed the snow from his hair, then narrowed his piercing eyes to scan the restaurant.

The sight of him garnered a different reaction than a few days ago. Maybe hiding away from the office made it easier to forget his charming demeanor and let the memory of his touch work its way out of my bloodstream. An addiction that I just needed to quit cold turkey. A total mistake.

"Can I help you?" Mrs. Baker leaned against the counter, a half-filled coffee pot in her hand.

"I'm just looking for—" his stare continued my way until it landed on my face. "Never mind. I found her. Thanks."

He nodded with a warm, gentle smile, then swaggered down the row of red vinyl booths toward me, his lips spreading into an even wider grin. I smiled back, my mouth betraying the negative thoughts that clouded my brain since the moment I saw him standing at the end of that conference room table Monday morning. Mrs. Baker stretched on her tiptoes and leaned over the cash register, nearly dropping the coffee pot as she watched him walk away. I shook my head. She winked back.

I slammed the top of my laptop closed and slid it into my bag avoiding any more eye contact with either of them. I'd tossed and turned all night dreading this meeting. Picturing the worst-case scenarios and waking up sweating. I couldn't believe I'd agreed to help him tear apart *The Herald*. It had been my life for years, even beyond my own column. The more I thought about it, the more it stoked a dangerous fire inside me. Despite Ben's suave air and amazingly powerful lips—that I had not been thinking about at all—I kind of wanted to send this grinch packing before he stole the Christmas I didn't even want to celebrate.

He slid into the seat across from me followed by the intoxicating scent of his cologne. The notes were tasteful yet matched him perfectly, bold and urban, like he'd just stepped out of a high-end downtown department store. Stores like that would be long decorated for the season by now. The intricate displays and immaculate designer trees would be lining every floor as old-time holiday classics drifted from the hidden speakers. Back in my college days, I spent hours wandering through the aisles, as the festive trimmings reminded me of home, but with a city flare. Like a perfect cross between who I was and who I one day could be.

"Thanks for meeting me outside the office. People seem to be pretty anxious with me around, so it's nice to get out and away from all that." He unbuttoned his jacket but kept it on, lacing his fingers on the tabletop in front of him and leaning forward. "Besides, this seems like a fun little place."

"And we make the best pie this side of the Mississippi." Ms. Baker appeared at the end of the table; her eyes glued to the new stranger. "Anything I can get you?"

"Yeah, I'll take a slice —" Ben glanced across the booth. I crossed my arms and glared back at him. "— or maybe I'll keep it simple and just take a coffee. Thanks."

"Sure thing, but you're missing out." She reached between us and flipped over a porcelain cup. She poured the hot coffee as she eyed my defiant stance and shook her head. She returned her focus to Ben. "If you need anything else, give me a holler. Sound good?"

"Absolutely. The coffee smells fantastic," he replied.

He beamed up at her, his warm eyes softening as he chuckled at her kindness. She smiled back and he flashed a glimpse of his perfect teeth, the sentiment seeming almost genuine. Eventually, she sauntered away leaving us to our business. Ben wrapped both palms around the steaming cup and arched his shoulders slightly forward as if absorbing the heat. My lips tried to smile, but I forced them to remain in a hard line, noting that he sat exactly the same way I did when the winter chill set in. The familiarity prickled in my brain. Maybe I was being too harsh.

"I'm sure you know why you have the office on edge. Everyone knows what your presence here means. Things are going to change, and I doubt anyone is going to like it." The words shot out my mouth like tiny darts aimed right at the bull's-eye that was his handsome face. So much for easing up on the harshness.

Ben sighed as his smile dissolved into a frown and he leaned back against the vinyl booth. "I know people aren't always thrilled to see me, but I'm not trying to be anyone's enemy. Honestly, this is just business. I figured if anyone would understand it would be you."

"Me? I have bills to pay too, you know."

"Of course, and I will do everything I can to keep people's jobs, but you're the youngest person on staff and you have experience in a bigger publication. I just thought you'd get that."

Any kindness I had left disappeared. "So you've been digging up on me?"

His left hand slipped from the coffee cup and he started to tap the table with his index finger. "It's on your resume, and I've looked into all the staff, not just you. It's my job. And speaking of jobs, I would like to know more about why you're working the advice column with your education and the internship you have under your belt?"

"Just because I love it. Best job ever." I grit my teeth and tried to hide any sarcasm by staring down into my lap.

"Okay… But if you love it so much, how come you have been trying to get a reporter position?"

I snapped my head back up. All humor faded from Ben's manner, leaving only his questioning stare that burned the top of my cheeks.

"I saw the stack of articles you had the other day,

plus Peter showed me a few of them. You're a great writer, Holly. He said you've been asking for a reporter job for a while."

"Well, thanks, but my time will come. One day. I just need to be patient."

He raised an eyebrow and kept staring until I looked away. "Really? With your talent, you could be at any national publication you wanted, not stuck at a tiny outfit like *The Herald*. You could be out there living a reporter's dream."

Through the window, the cheery sunshine glistened on the pristine blanket of snow accumulating on the side of the street. Another charming day in Havenbrook. Back at my old office in the city, if I looked out I could watch all of Kansas City go by. The hustle and bustle of the busy newsroom. The urgency of the next edition. The energy of it seeped from my memory and lit in my bones. I slid my hands beneath my thighs and bit down on the inside of my cheek.

"That's pretty precocious coming from you. I mean, are you living your dream, Ben? Ruining people's lives and destroying the careers that people have spent their lives working toward?"

"Of course not." He blinked for a second, slow and meticulous, then gazed out the sunlit window. "I don't enjoy breaking things down, but sometimes you need to cut off a few dead branches for the tree to grow. Personally, I'd prefer to be the one building things up instead of knocking them down, but Concorde is the family business, and sometimes you have to do what you have to do."

I released my tense shoulders and let out a sigh. "Yeah, family can make things tricky."

"Interesting comment. Does that have anything to do with David Brighton?" He shook his head and leaned back across the table, pinning me with his inquisitive gaze again. "When I was going through the financials, I noticed his name as the editor-in-chief before Peter. Any relation?"

I opened my mouth to speak, but nothing came out. Pulling my arms in closer to my body, I cleared my throat. "Yeah, something like that."

He hung in silence, the eager quiver of his top lip exposing his need to say something and the struggle he had to keep his mouth closed, waiting for me to elaborate. But I wouldn't. An old reporter trick. Let the silence draw out the truth. Very clever. But magicians aren't very mysterious when the audience knows their tricks.

After several uncomfortable minutes of the staring game, he sat back and drained the coffee cup with a loud gulp. "Okay, Holly, I've tried to be nice, but you clearly don't like me and that's fine. But I still need to do my job and I thought if you were willing to help, I could salvage a lot more of the paper than doing this on my own. I know you don't like this. I don't like this. But it's going to happen with or without you." He re-clasped the buttons on his coat and stood by the table as he slipped a ten-dollar bill out of his pocket and placed it under the empty cup. My entire body burned. I expected it to be anger, but it sure seemed more like embarrassment. What had I done?

He took a few steps toward the door, then halted and spun back around on his perfectly polished dress shoes.

"For what it's worth, I was excited to see you walk into that boardroom. I felt so lucky to have met a woman so intelligent and charming, not once but twice. It seemed like fate was trying to help me out, but I guess I was just being hopeful. Thank you for your time."

He raced to the entrance and nodded at Ms. Baker as he walked out. I winced at the tinkling of the bell as the door slammed shut behind him. *Why did I need to be so hostile?* I crossed my arms on the table and dropped my forehead on them, inhaling the lemon scent of the sanitized tabletop. What a complete disaster. Maybe I needed to lose this angry persona and find that amazing girl from the bar too.

CHAPTER FIVE

$\mathcal{A}$lmost all of Havenbrook passed by as I hid against the brick wall near the bank. They waved and shone their carefree friendly grins as they shuffled down the snowy sidewalk, while I forced myself to smile back, my meeting with Ben still plaguing me. Ben with his dreamy hair and sexy quiver to his top lip when he spewed those words, assuming he knew all about me. But if he was so wrong, why did his assumptions still bother me almost five hours later?

A shock of red hair sticking out from a woolen beanie drifted by and snapped me out of my annoying thoughts.

"Claire, wait up." I peeled away from the wall and leaped two giant steps down the sidewalk after her, then clamped my hand on her shoulder.

She whirled around and gasped. "Jeez, Holly, are you trying to give me a heart attack?"

She clasped her mittened hand across her chest as small puffs of her breath hung in the frigid air.

"Sorry, I really need to talk to you about Ben."

"Ben? You mean the super-hot guy you kissed at the bar and turned out to be your boss's boss? That Ben?" Claire shot a naughty wink, then continued to scurry down the sidewalk.

I rushed along beside her avoiding eye contact and the small patches of ice along the concrete. "Well, clearly, that was a mistake. I met him for lunch today to talk about the paper, but I think I made things worse."

"I'm sure it's not as bad as you think. What did you say?"

I thrust my hands in my pockets and stared down at my feet. "Pretty much everything that came out of my mouth was a problem. I basically argued with everything he said and chased him out before he even finished his coffee."

"Yikes." Claire halted and grabbed my arm, yanking me back a step. She stared me down in the concerned way she always did when I put my foot firmly into my mouth. "That bad, huh? What did he say?"

"First, he mentioned the change to digital, which you know is just going to destroy *The Herald*."

She shook her head and started walking again. "Maybe not. But keep going."

"And then, he started talking about my writing and how I should move into the city and become a reporter."

"Well, that's good, right?" she said. "It's exactly what I've been telling you to do, anyway."

I locked eyes on the giant wreath hanging over the doors of St. Michael's Church, just behind Claire's head. I stared harder as a strange tickle started in my throat.

"But that's not what you told him, was it?"

I heard her sigh but still couldn't look at her face. I shook my head. "No, I kept right on going. I'll be surprised if I even have a job by tomorrow morning."

"Seriously, Holly?" Claire stopped walking and tugged my chin down to her. "I know you've been going through a lot lately, with Fletcher and all, but if you don't stop being so dramatic you're going to end up hurting yourself more than that jerk ever could."

"I know, but you know how much *The Herald* means to me. I can't just let somebody come in here and ruin everything. It would be catastrophic."

"Yeah, but at some point, you're going to have to let it go."

Her words stung like needles, delivering the harsh medicine I so desperately needed. "I need to apologize to him, don't I? Like possibly full out groveling?"

She nodded and squeezed my arm through her mitten. A comforting jolt of warmth sparked up my arm. "It might be just fine. I'm sure if you explain why you were upset, he'd understand. He actually seemed like a pretty reasonable guy that night at Danny's."

"Maybe. But how am I going to be able to convince him to stop messing with the paper and everyone else's lives here?"

Claire shrugged and dropped my arm as she continued up the sidewalk. "I don't know. Perhaps if he understood how much the paper means to Havenbrook and what people are really like here versus big cities, he'd reconsider."

The spark of an idea flashed in the back of my brain, growing larger and brighter by the second. "Yeah. You might be right, Claire. That's exactly what I need to do."

"Did you want to come for dinner? I'm sure Austin would love to see you, and I'm trying a new Mexican recipe that's going to be way too much food for the two of us. Besides, I want to show you the dress I got for the fundraising gala tomorrow. And don't forget, we are supposed to help set up just after lunch."

Details formed and clicked in place like puzzle pieces. A puzzle that seemed to look a lot like Christmas. If anyone could make Ben see this town for what it was, it would definitely be me.

"Holly?" Claire waved her hand in front of my face, barely missing my nose "What about dinner? Did you want to come?"

I shook my head as the final parts slid into place. "Sorry, I have plans all of a sudden. Or more like a plan."

Claire crossed her arms and narrowed her stare. "What are you up to?"

"Don't worry," I nodded my head and smiled broadly until her concerned face cracked into a laugh. "It will be fine, but do you think your husband would mind if I borrowed a few of his things?"

CHAPTER SIX

*T*he night sky settled around me, inky black and a little ominous, as doubts about my master plan crept into my brain. Everything seemed perfect when I left my house, but as I stood in the hotel parking lot with its instrumental holiday songs blaring through the front speakers, I considered turning around the way I came and curling up in my comfy bed until the new year. I'd already made things as bad as I could, why risk making it worse?

Except the knot in my stomach from my botched lunch meeting kept squeezing tighter and giving up might cause it to rip me apart. No turning back now. I took a deep breath and let it out slowly as I pulled open the door of the Starlight Inn.

"Good evening, welcome to the Star— Hey, Holly what are you doing here?"

I flinched at the recognition. Robbie Benson, clean-cut and all-business in his purple vest and gold name tag, launched a wide grin at me from across the lobby. The beauty of small towns was that you knew everybody. But the curse was also that you knew everybody. In Robbie's case, all the way back to kindergarten.

"Hey, I didn't realize you worked here." I did. "How is your mom doing?" Which I already knew.

"Better, she's back in remission, so that's something to be grateful for."

Tugging my tote bag closer to my body, I marched up to the counter and delivered my best courteous smile. "Well, that's amazing. And just in time for the holidays too."

Robbie's shoulders relaxed as a warm grin spread across his face. "Absolutely. We couldn't ask for better timing."

I stretched up on my toes and leaned over the counter. "So, is there any chance you'd be able to tell me what room Benjamin Concorde is staying in?"

His smile turned into a playful smirk. "Holly Brighton, are you stalking our guests? I might have to call the sheriff."

"Of course not." I forced a laugh, but it came out more nervous than I'd hoped. "It's strictly business. He works for the parent company that owns the paper. He already knows I'm coming, he just rushed out of the office so quickly I forgot to ask him his room number."

"Hold on, have we slipped back a few decades or can you not just text him?"

Think, Holly, think. "I…"

Robbie slapped his hand against the wooden

counter and threw his head back with a guttural laugh. "I'm just messing with you. He's in 204."

I eased away from the counter, shrunk my neck into the collar of my coat, and ran for the stairs. "Thanks," I yelled over my shoulder as I bounded up the first flight.

Walking slow, I focused on catching my breath before I reached Ben's door. I'd already left enough bad impressions for one day. The television roared inside. It sounded like a newscast. Boring. Didn't he get enough of this at work every day? Maybe this wasn't really a good idea. Maybe I could just go and he'd never know I was here. Unless, of course, Robbie decided to mention it to him in the morning. I grit my teeth and shivered. That would be so much worse.

Another deep breath and I rapped my knuckles against the old oak door.

One second… Two seconds… Three seconds… Four. No answer. Fine by me.

I turned on my heel and rushed back down the hallway toward the stairs and my escape.

"Holly?"

I slammed to a stop, nearly falling over my own feet as Ben's deep voice called out my name. My shoulders eased, but I quickly tensed them back up. No. It didn't matter how sexily my name rolled off his tongue. I was here for one purpose only.

Plastering on my best small-town hospitality smile, I whirled around and strutted back toward Ben's door, exuding as much confidence as I could muster.

"Ben, so you are home. I mean, in your room. I guess this isn't really your home, now is it?" Seriously? For someone who worked with words all day, I didn't have a clue how to use them. My arm twitched, aching to hide my face in my hand, but I fought it down and kept it locked by my side.

He narrowed his questioning eyes then leaned against the open door, arms crossed. "Yeah, not really home. But for the amount I travel, it might as well be. What are you doing here?"

The soft scent of cucumber mint soap wafted through the hall. Ben's wet hair clung to his forehead and a small droplet of water trickled down his cheek. Instead of his tailored suit, he'd changed into a black T-shirt and a dark washed pair of jeans, his sleeves tugging just enough against his toned biceps. The whole look fit him well. Too well.

"I..." I peeled my eyes away from the contours of his shirt to ease my tongue and aid the words to flow. "I feel like we might have gotten off on the wrong foot today."

He frowned, but his eyes danced with curiosity. "I would say so."

"You asked for my help, and I didn't provide it. But, if you really want to know what *The Herald* means to Havenbrook, then you need to experience it. Get out of your closet-sized hotel room and be a part of the action."

"Sounds a bit like a sales pitch, Ms. Brighton."

Ms. Brighton? I really must've screwed things up today.

"No, just an opportunity. Besides, what else were you going to do tonight?"

His face furrowed for a second and then he shrugged, the frown melting away into the dim light of the hallway. "I guess I better take you up on your offer then. Just hold on a second and I'll grab my coat."

"Oh, and you'll probably need these." I slipped the tote bag off my shoulder and held it open.

He pulled the scarf, hat, and mitts I borrowed from Austin out of the bag. "Am I going to regret this?"

"Maybe. But we'll never know for sure if you don't come with me."

CHAPTER SEVEN

*S*trands of white lights twinkled above our heads and led us down the bustling street. Red bows dotted the pastel-colored awnings as we passed, while boughs of evergreens swooped between the candy cane striped tents lining the snowy sidewalks.

"C'mon, Mr. Concorde, we're almost there." I glanced over my shoulder and beckoned with my gloved fingers.

Ben rolled his eyes but continued to follow me as I twisted our way through the crowd toward the town square and the heart of the Havenbrook Christmas Market. With his hair tucked underneath Austin's beanie, he almost blended in with the locals. Except he'd never be one of them. Ben stood too rigid for a small town. Too proper. Even in the door of his hotel room, hair a mess and wearing denim, he still screamed of the city. Of traffic and subway stations. High rises and billboards. So why did the thought of him seem exhilarating instead of exhausting?

Near the edge of the square, I slowed, taking in a deep breath of cool winter air. A crisp, clean taste skated over my tongue, and memories of years of perfect nights like this one swirled in my head. The crunch of footfalls whispered behind me as Ben's warm breath rustled the hair near my neck. I shivered but shook it off.

"I thought you hated all this Christmas stuff?" he said as he stepped beside me and put his hands on his hips.

I glanced around the square. So many happy faces that I'd known for my whole life, glowing bright with rosy frostbitten cheeks. "What makes you say that? Who hates Christmas?"

"You gave me that vibe when we met." Ben's face scrunched up in a failed attempt to hide his amused grin. "Plus, that night you announced to the bar that you hated it."

My stomach churned and I rubbed my hand over my face. I peeked out from between my fingers as the recollection came speeding back. "Seriously?"

"I wouldn't worry, it was too loud in there for anyone to hear you anyway."

"Anyone, but you, I guess."

Ben laughed. Light and airy. I must have been a bigger mess than I remembered.

I stared down at the well-trodden sidewalk, studying the imprints of the various boot grips that had come before us. "Well, I didn't mean it ... exactly.

It hasn't been the best year for me and, well, you kind of came along when I was having a rough time."

He tucked his mittened fingers under my chin and tilted my head up to meet his gaze. The playfulness from the prior moment melted as his dark eyes softened and drew me in like a comforting cup of caramel hot chocolate. "I hope things get better. I don't want to be the cause of any more trouble for you."

"We'll see." My throat tightened, and I slipped out of his gentle grip to stare off toward the skating circle in front of the giant Christmas tree. "Now, I didn't bring you here to talk about me. I need to show you something."

I jerked my head to the left and started weaving through the crowd again. Along the side of city hall, full spreads of *The Herald* hung in giant wooden frames, their supporting chains wrapped in silver and gold ribbons.

"This is the holiday edition from 1984." I pointed at the black-and-white photo of handmade candy canes underneath the vintage *Herald* masthead, then slipped around the frame to the next one. "And here is 1956 and 1957."

The images of Christmas trees and sleigh rides burst off the pages. Headlines in their bold fonts followed by uplifting articles in their neat little rows. Just as they always were. As they always should be.

Ben stuffed his hands in his pockets and studied the pages, his eyes flitting back and forth as he read every word. "What is all this?"

"Moments captured in time and lovingly archived by the citizens of Havenbrook."

Ben coughed at the sentiment as his left eyebrow arched up. A puff of steam from his breath swirled around his head.

"Or if you like a more straightforward answer, this is an exhibit of all the year end issues of *The Herald* as far back as they could find them. They are missing most of the ones from the early 1800s, but almost every other one is here. Framed and preserved, then put on display every Christmas for the whole town, or anyone who happens to come through, to see."

"That's incredible." He crossed his arms over his chest and leaned back on his heels to take in the entire exhibit. "They've kept them all in amazing condition."

"Yes. *The Herald* means a lot to Havenbrook. To me. It's one of the few things that unifies everyone here. Ever steady. I don't know where you're from, Ben—"

"Chicago."

"Sure." I shook my head. Just as I suspected. "But small towns are different. They stand for tradition and revel in consistency."

I kept walking through the exhibit, running my fingertips over the frames as I passed and letting them swing slightly in my wake.

"Did you know if you walk into Mrs. Baker's diner on any Saturday morning, you will find every single person with their head down in *The Herald*? Every sports team has a sponsorship from the paper and any athlete that goes pro gives us exclusive access for their first interview. People maintain their subscriptions as part of their wills and pass it on to their children."

I rounded through the late 70s section and lingered in front of a familiar headline. My heart pumped harder in my chest as I struggled to breathe. I closed my eyes as the faded black and white smile beamed at me. Without looking, I remembered every detail of the photo. The curve of his brow. The tiny scar to the left of his nose. He looked so young then. No wrinkles or the worry lines that would soon etch themselves across his forehead. Pride and ambition, but with a warmth that melted even the coolest critic. *The Herald Announces New Editor-In-Chief, David Brighton.* I knew the words without looking. Each one seared across my heart. "For some people, *The Herald* means home."

A chill flitted across my cheek as Ben's shadow cast over me. "Seems pretty important to you too."

"It is." I swallowed hard and fluttered my eyes back open. "I owe you an apology. You asked for my help and instead of being honest I chose to be a little...well...hostile."

Ben snickered behind me. "Really? I hadn't noticed."

Peeling my gaze away from the frame, I whirled around, my face right against Ben's chest. I gasped, and stumbled a step backward, not expecting to be nearly so close. A warm rush bubbled in my veins, but I pushed the feeling down. "That wasn't fair to you. You're just trying to do your job."

"And you are doing yours. I wish you'd been more

open with me, but I get it. You really care and it shows. Conviction and passion are not things to be ashamed of." He lowered his head as his dark stare locked on mine. Just as quickly the shadows flitted into the night and a softness eked in. "However, I was really looking forward to Mrs. Baker's pie so I think you might owe me a slice."

"Very funny. But I'm serious, how do you think the town is going to take *The Herald* going digital? They couldn't exactly have exhibits like this."

"No, I suppose they can't." He nodded and scanned over the years of history tied in metallic bows. A concerned frown grew stronger on his deep, red lips. "Except sometimes history is just that—history. The paper needs to generate more ad revenue. It can't be bleeding money like it has over the past few years. Digital could be a way to save the paper from an even worse fate. How do you think Havenbrook would feel if we had to close *The Herald* instead?"

The reality froze me in my boots. I'd visualized a world in which the paper went digital and that had been bleak, but I never imagined that closing the paper entirely would be an option. I wrapped my arms across my chest, then wandered away from the exhibit toward the bustle of the market again. People flitted in front of me. Blurs of festive colors moving far faster than I had time to process. Clenching my jacket sleeves in my hands, I shivered as the cold December breeze finally seeped into my bones and froze me to my core.

"Trust me, it's not something I would want to do."

Ben's voice drifted toward me but still seemed miles away. "But sometimes it's the way it is. I have to do my job too, even if it's not always fun."

I dug my fingertips into my arms and sighed. "So, why do you do it then?"

"Do what?"

"This job? If you don't like having to deal with these kinds of things, why don't you make a change? You're a Concorde. Your family owns the company. I'm sure if you wanted to do something different, you could."

Snow crunched behind me as he stepped up on my left. He didn't try to steal my attention, just stared straight out into the crowd as the night washed over him. The icy breeze nipped at his nose as a calmness cloaked his expression.

"You're not wrong. I do think about it sometimes. What it would be like to not live out of a suitcase for six months out of the year. To slow down and maybe stay somewhere longer than a week at a time. But my family depends on me. My mother runs the main office in Chicago, my sisters head the satellite offices on either coast, and my father spends his time between all three. They need someone in the field and as the youngest, I sort of fell into the role."

"And you get to be the sacrifice."

He chuckled, but the humor left his lips flat and jaded. "I guess I am."

I released the iron grip on my arms and nudged him with my shoulder. "See, was that so hard? Maybe there is a soul under that expensive suit after all."

"Maybe." He swayed toward me and bumped his shoulder into mine.

The chill in my limbs melted away as I tipped slightly to the right and my harsh frown slipped away. I chuckled softly and the sound teased a smile from Ben.

"Now you know about me, but I don't seem to know much about you. How is that fair?" he asked.

"What did you want to know?" A loaded question. A deadly one if wielded properly. But maybe he could be trusted. Or maybe I'd unleashed a whole mess of trouble.

"Well…"

He rubbed his hand under his chin as his inquisitive eyes rolled toward the length of plastic candy canes strung in rows above our heads.

"Is it really that tough?"

He scanned over my face, his smile widening. "Don't want to waste this opportunity?"

"You shouldn't. You never know—"

The never-ending stream of people flowing behind Ben's head came into focus. Two familiar faces solidified in the crowd, grinning and giggling like teenagers. Fletcher and Dierdre. Why now? Bile rose in my throat. I grabbed Ben's arm and swung him around so we backed against the swarm of market goers, then tucked in closer to him.

He glanced back over his shoulder and almost immediately the light of recognition sparked across his face. "I'm assuming that means you two still aren't on good terms?"

I shook my head. "Not exactly. I'm pretty sure that's never going to happen."

His head swiveled following Fletcher, then swooped back down at my head cowered against his shoulder.

"All clear."

I exhaled sharply, and the feeling returned to my body. My numb fingers released their clutch on Ben's jacket near the zipper on his firm chest. "Sorry."

"It's fine. My ex is a nightmare too. How long were you two together?"

"Too long, I guess. Or at least I would have hoped he'd broke up with me before he started dating someone else."

"Ouch." Ben's face scrunched up. "Sounds like you're better off. Maybe it wasn't meant to be?"

I craned my neck and tried to get my blood flow back. The shock drained from my muscles and was replaced quickly with a new tension. One that made my knees quake. "Sounds a bit spiritual for a practical guy like you."

"Not really. If your processes are failing, it could be time to liquidate and move on. Spending too much time and money on bad investments just puts you in a worse position. Sometimes it's better just to start over."

"Sounds great, but it's not always that easy. How many times have you started over?"

His brows furrowed and his mouth opened, but only his breath came out.

"I thought so." I closed my eyes for a moment and

took a deep, calming breath. "It's admirable advice. Thanks for trying."

Ben shoved his hands in his pockets and stared at the ground. "I guess I've never really lost anything that meant that much to me."

"Like *The Herald* means to Havenbrook."

I rocked back on my heels, as the words burned on my tongue. I shouldn't have said that, but it just flowed out before I could stop it. My impeccable timing almost uncontrollable. Too late now.

The melodic chime of carols wafted through the market, hiding the silence growing fast between us. I'd orchestrated this outing to help convince Ben that *The Herald* needed to stay as it was, but instead, I'd only made a bigger mess. Shown him how big of a wreck I really was. How would he even consider listening to me now? I glanced around the square. The bright lights sparked a new idea.

"So, Mr. Concorde, how are you at ice skating?"

CHAPTER EIGHT

"Oh no, you don't." I pushed down on my left foot and lunged forward with all my strength. Wind whipped my hair against my face as I glided faster and faster around the frozen pond, Ben's gray wool jacket less than an arm's length away.

He looked back over his shoulder. "Did you really think that challenging me to a race would end well for you? I'm a little competitive if you haven't noticed."

I dug each foot deeper into the ice as I skated, forcing my legs forward. His long gait could only help him so much. His stride was too choppy. Sure, that might help with a quick start, but it wouldn't hold him for a long distance. The rented skates wobbled around my ankles but I pressed on, determined not to let him beat me.

The gap between us closed. A few more strides. Gritting my teeth, I gave it one last push to sail past him. I spun around on my toe and skated backward for my victory lap. I pumped my arms in the air.

"Woohoo! Take that, Ben."

He tossed his head back and slowed down to drift lazily around the skating circle in front of me. His deep laugh echoed throughout the square.

"Impressive. Seven years of hockey and I get taken down by a small-town girl. My father is going to be pissed when he finds out his money didn't prepare me for battle."

"Well, I'm definitely not one to be underestimated."

He dropped his chin and lunged toward me, gripping my jacket at my waist. "I'm starting to figure that out."

The air thickened. Heavy. Pressing on my chest and making it hard to breathe. Ben mimicked my reaction as his breath caught in his throat. Only the chill of the night remained between us—except I couldn't seem to feel it.

"Thanks for giving me a second chance," I whispered, low and delicate to not ruin the moment. "I shouldn't have been so rude at the cafe. It's not how I normally am, I just get a bit emotional about things sometimes. Things that are important to me."

He brushed my hair off my shoulder and inched closer. "It's not a bad thing. You can't teach people to be passionate about what they care about."

His words rolled off his tongue and warmed my cheeks. I didn't hate him. It would be easier if I did, but I couldn't. I held onto his solid biceps and stood up straighter. The distance between our bodies closed inch by precious inch. Ben's eyes widened, but instead of pulling back, he held my waist tighter, drawing me in. An odd sensation pulsed through me as I melted into him and craved so much more.

"Look, Mom, he's going to kiss her under the mistletoe," a tiny voice shouted, cutting through the ambiance.

I turned to my left. A little girl, with two braids sticking out from underneath her fuzzy pink beanie, smiled at us with a dark gap where her top front tooth should be. Her mother gave me a shrug and pushed the little girl forward and out of the way.

"Ha. That's ridiculous." I let go of his strong arms and spun around to skate toward the side of the pond. "My feet are killing me in these borrowed skates. I think I'm done."

I shook my head and flopped onto the long bench beside the ice. Ben plunked down beside me and looked me over, quickly ripping the laces open on his skates.

"Why don't I grab some hot chocolate while you return these?" he said, passing me the snow-covered blades.

I nodded and leaned back as he walked away. He glanced over his shoulder and smiled until I waved at him. My lips started to pucker and the image of our kiss at Danny's flashed through my brain, mixing with the ones I'd found myself imagining in my dreams. What was going on? He worked for my employer. He was practically my boss. So, why did I suddenly want him back here on the bench with me?

After returning the skates, Ben appeared at my side with a steaming paper cup. "Here you go."

"Thanks." I took a quick sip and let the smooth liquid soothe my dry throat. "I should probably be getting you back to your hotel. I'm sure you have work in the morning and I hear the executives at head office are a bit conservative."

He narrowed his stare. "Is that how you see me?"

"Sometimes. But I think I might be able to be convinced otherwise."

"Then my master plan is working. I knew I could blend in."

I laughed. "You definitely don't blend in. Not even in that hat."

He frowned and adjusted the beanie on his head, his dark hair peeking out from underneath the sides.

We strode beneath the strings of white lights leading back to Main Street. The last few vendors busily packed up their wares, shoving items into boxes and rushing away. It must be later than I thought.

"So, how exactly were you able to find my hotel room?" Ben asked as he lined up and tossed his cup into a nearby garbage can. A perfect shot. He pumped his fist in the air at his victory.

"It's not like it was that hard. There are only three decent inns in Havenbrook." I shrugged and tossed my own empty cup into the same garbage can. *Swish.* I smirked. "Besides, the Starlight is the only place in town that offers us a corporate discount."

"Well, that is some pretty good investigative work

there, Ms. Brighton." He stopped walking and leaned in closer, staring down into my eyes. The rich scent of hot chocolate still clung to his breath. Sweet and warm. "You really would make a great reporter."

"Maybe. But that's not my job, at least not at *The Herald*. So, why bother talking about it?"

I unlocked my gaze from Ben's and looked back toward the skating pond. A fresh batch of snow had started to drift silently between the buildings flanking the festive street.

"Peter told me you've been gunning for a reporter position for months. There are so many opportunities out there. Why not go for what you want? I really don't understand."

I swallowed against the lump growing in my throat. "Because it's complicated. Havenbrook and *The Herald* are my home. Sometimes I do miss working for a bigger outlet. The excitement of the city. But I can't just abandon this place."

"Havenbrook is amazing, but you won't be able to follow your reporting dreams here. Even if Peter gave you the job you asked for, it would be extremely limited on what you could achieve. Maybe your old internship would take you back at an entry level, just to get your foot in the door again."

I sighed and glanced up at the sky. The snowflakes fell on my eyelashes, creating a haze over my vision. "Because I wasn't there long enough to matter. I accepted that internship at the Kansas City Star, but only a few months after I started my dad got sick and I had to come back. My mom died when I was a baby and there wasn't anyone around to take care of him."

I blinked away the snow and shoved my hands in my pockets, pulling my arms tight to my sides. A cool, wintry wind whipped through the empty market stalls, swirling the snowflakes around my feet with every hurried step.

Ben walked along beside me in silence until he finally said softly, "I'm sorry, Holly. I didn't know."

"Why would you? It isn't a front-page news kind of story. I came back and started my life over again here."

"And your dad?"

I swallowed hard and blinked twice to avoid the inevitable tears from falling. "Three months. That's all he had left."

Ben wrapped his hand over my shoulder then quickly pulled his hand away. "I'm so sorry."

I swept my finger along my lashes and forced the painful memories back into their box in the deepest parts of my brain. "It happens."

"Well, if you ever change your mind, I could be a huge asset for your career."

"Oh yeah," I said, with a touch of intrigue.

"Yeah, I have a ton of contacts in the industry, not just at Concorde but other publications as well. And —" Ben rested the back of his hand against my cheek. The heat soothed the still fresh wounds and I fell into his touch. "I'm sure any paper would love to have someone like you working for them. We're lucky to have you working for us."

"Thanks. I—"

The world plunged into darkness as the lights of the markets flicked off. I tugged away from Ben's touch and looked around. The street was deserted and the skating circle lay calm and barren.

"I guess we've outstayed our welcome."

The star-studded sky gave way to the neon sign of the Starlight Inn. Like the falling snow, we'd drifted here, slow and aimless, until our feet found the front door. The harsh artificial light of the lobby called, but the moonlit glow of outside wrapped us like a blanket and refused to let us go. Or maybe I'd just lost the feeling in my nose and toes.

"Here we are, Mr. Concorde. Safe and sound."

He glanced toward the front door and then back at me, still standing firm on the sidewalk. "Thanks. I think I really got to know Havenbrook a lot better."

"Yeah. I love it here. Plus, when it snows like this, it's kind of beautiful."

His eyes narrowed on mine. "It sure is."

Electricity pulsed through my body, awakening parts of my heart that had fallen asleep. Except, he couldn't really be the Prince Charming of my fairytale. We'd never be a happy ending.

"Um … that was—"

"Super cheesy. I'm so sorry." He emitted a low sexy growl and grabbed the back of his neck. His teeth caught on his bottom lip. The bright white mesmerizing against the dark red under the moonlight. A warmth rushed through me fighting against the cold night air and I jerked as I unintentionally bit down on my own lip, sending a jolt of pain through my chin.

"I should probably go." I pointed back toward town but didn't move except to fumble my house keys in my hands. My empty house.

"Yeah, work in the morning. Of course. Thank you for saving me from a night of bad television and spreadsheets."

"You're welcome. I kind of owed you one, anyway."

He tilted his head and blinked.

"But before I go." I cleared my throat. "That first night. At Danny's. I never thanked you for helping me deal with Fletcher. I should have."

"No problem. I did spill a drink on you, so I had to make sure we were even. But after tonight, I think you're one up on me."

"Okay." I turned on my heel but stopped. "But why did you do it? I know about the drink and all, but it was a bit of a risk. And you didn't really have to."

"I guess I like fixing things more than breaking them. Besides, if I remember correctly, it was you who kissed me."

Flames licked my skin as the memory of the night flashed back in my head. Flickers of embarrassment and excitement. Still confusing to me several days later. "True. Sorry about that."

"Don't apologize. It was the best welcome I've had my entire career."

"It was a pretty great kiss." One of the better ones

I'd had. Maybe even the best. Or maybe I just remembered it that way. Then the memory dissipated as I faced him again.

"That was before I knew you were my boss. But, depending on how your restructuring goes, you might not be for long."

"Hey. I will do whatever I can to protect *The Herald*." He took my hand and caressed it between his own, then placed his forehead against mine. "And you."

His lips rested so close to mine. I tasted them in my mind and ached for another bite.

"I believe you." I pushed up on my tiptoes and grazed my lips against his cold cheek, the barely there stubble scratching against my skin. "See you tomorrow."

CHAPTER NINE

*T*he sunlight shimmered off the pristine white banks that flanked the sidewalk on the way to the office. Each flake a twinkling diamond shining on my every step. A whole new, glorious world since yesterday. I sipped my mocha latte, letting the rich chocolate slide down my throat and warm me from the inside. A magnificent morning that would hopefully bring a fantastic day. Ben had promised to protect the paper the best he could, and the words played on a sultry repeat in my head from the moment they left his deep, delicious lips.

I took another sip and shook my head. I shouldn't be thinking about him that way. He controlled my career. My destiny. Any sort of feelings for him would be a huge mistake. I just wish someone could relate that to my dream brain before it worked overtime last night.

"Good morning, Doris," I said as I breezed through

the front door of the office and stomped the snow off the toes of my boots.

"Good morning to you too, Holly. You seem in an exceptionally chipper mood this morning." Her befuddled look followed me across the lobby.

"A wonderful night followed by a good sleep. How could I not be in a great mood?" And for once it wasn't a lie or a polite put-on. For the first time in the last several weeks, I finally felt hopeful. Like I could take on the world.

I slipped off my jacket as I scurried through the maze of cubicles toward my desk. Before I managed to duck into my cube, the boardroom door opened at the end of the hall. Peter and Ben filed out, heading my direction.

"Good morning, Holly." Jenkins scanned me over. "Don't you typically work from home on Thursdays?"

I stiffened for a moment, my back stick straight. "Sometimes, yeah. But I had some things to take care of here today."

"Just make sure you hit those deadlines." He waggled his finger at me as his stern face broke into a smile. "You've never missed one yet, and I would hate for you to break your streak."

Ben cleared his throat and moved to Jenkin's side. The soft casualness of last night's demeanor had been smoothed back into its urban, hard style. Except this time his dazzling warm grin didn't quite match his cool exterior. "A pleasure to see you again, Ms. Brighton."

He nodded politely, then stared up at me through his dark lashes.

I swallowed down the ridiculous bubble of excitement threatening to burst from my mouth in a completely unprofessional giggle. I glanced up at the ceiling. "You too, Mr. Concorde. I hope you have been enjoying your stay."

He took a step forward, closing the distance between us. "Of course. I'm beginning to see how much Havenbrook has to offer."

"We have that conference call at nine in my office, Ben. Don't want to keep your father waiting." Jenkins sidled along beside us casting a questioning look for me to Ben and back again.

"Of course," Ben straightened his suit jacket and checked that the buttons were secure. "Wouldn't want that."

He followed Peter down the hall toward his office but glanced back to catch me watching him walk away. I smacked my hand against my forehead and dragged it down the side of my face. This was stupid. I was being stupid. Like a giddy teenager instead of the competent woman I knew I was. This, whatever this was, needed to stop. He controlled my career, and being unprofessional wasn't going to help anything.

I rushed the rest of the way to my cubicle and flung my coat over the back of my chair. A shaft of rainbow light painted across my desk. I glanced up at my desktop monitor.

A small crystal snowflake hung off the edge of my screen. I slipped its royal blue ribbon from its perch and dangled it in front of my face. The morning sun streaming through the windows on the far wall caught the edges and cast colored beams all around my cube.

I pulled at the tiny ring of paper looped around the ribbon.

For taking a second chance.

I replaced the snowflake on my monitor and peered over my half walls at Peter's office. Ben smiled as he nodded my direction and slowly closed the door. I flopped into my desk chair and pulled my laptop from my bag. If I didn't focus on work, who knew what trouble my brain would get into.

The words flowed fast. Much quicker than they had in months. Inspiration fired out of my fingers like electricity. A superhero of syntax. I polished off five *Ask Holly* letters and still managed to write a brand-new article without even taking a break to breathe.

But the search for a synonym to 'repugnant' slowed down my process. As I surveyed the list of options, a strange buzzing noise rattled my concentration. The noise stopped. I glanced around, shook my head, and went back to my thesaurus search. The noise buzzed again.

I listened for a second, then reached down into my purse and pulled out my cell phone.

"Hey Claire, what's up?" I asked as I spun my chair away from my desk and stretched out my stiff legs.

"I've been calling for like three hours. It's not like you not to pick up."

"Sorry, I was just in the writing zone today. I don't know what happened, but I'll take it."

"Does it have anything to do with why you absconded from my house with my husband's warmest mittens?"

"Maybe." I teased. "But I will get them back to you soon."

"No rush. But when are you going to get to the hall? I thought you said you had time to help set up?"

I glanced at the time on the bottom left of my monitor. Already 2:19. What happened to my morning? My stomach growled, asking the same question.

"I'm so sorry. I didn't notice the time. But if you give me about a half hour, I'll be there."

"Only if you can. But I'd really appreciate it. There's still so much to do and I need to get home to get ready."

"Be right there."

I hung up the phone and shoved it back into my purse. I shut my laptop and snatched up my coat as I lunged toward the cubicle entrance. A silhouette hovered over my escape.

"Leaving already?"

The coat slipped from my fingers and landed in a pile on the floor. Ben gracefully swept it up in his arm and handed it back.

"Thanks." My fingers lingered next to his, just like his gaze hesitated to leave my face.

"Yeah, I have somewhere I have to be. And I'm late."

He kept smiling, but a shadow fell over his expression. "Well, I won't stop you then. But what about later? I really wanted to talk to you some more." He leaned closer and dropped his lips close to my ear, his voice a seductive whisper. "I really had a great time last night."

"Me too." I slipped right to put some distance between us. "But I can't. There's a fundraiser for the children's hospital wing and I promised I'd be there. That's actually where I'm going now, to help set up the event."

"Okay. But maybe I could call later or something?" A strange new look overthrew his flirty demeanor.

"Is everything alright, Ben?" I rested my hand on his arm and he seemed to steady. "Wait. I can do one better. Here, if you don't have anything else going on, why don't you come to the fundraiser?"

I spun around and rummaged through my purse to find the tattered ticket envelope. I slid the red and white card stock tickets out into my fist. One of them was supposed to be Fletcher's, but there wasn't any chance that he'd go anywhere near me now. I held the extra ticket out toward Ben. "The paper sponsors the event, so I'm sure it would be fine if you came."

"But I—"

"It's a bit fancier, but one of your posh city suits

would be just fine. You'll probably be better dressed than half the men there."

He puffed his chest and stood up straighter, brushing invisible lint from his lapels. "So, you do like this look."

"Don't get too far ahead of yourself, Mr. Concorde. I just said you would blend in fine."

"What's the point of blending in when you can stand out?"

I tapped him gently on the chest and brushed close past with my coat and bags. "Badly misquoting other writers won't impress me. But meet me at The Havenbrook Museum at the end of Virginia Street. 7 o'clock. I might let you try again."

I hurried down the hall, fighting the goofy grin trying to plaster itself on my lips. From behind me, Ben yelled, "I'll be there."

CHAPTER TEN

"*What?*" Claire's head jerked forward. "You invited him here? That Ben guy you kissed at the bar? The one who owns *the Herald?*"

"Shhh." I glanced over my shoulder. A few couples swayed on the dance floor, while everyone else huddled in private groups gossiping and cackling the night away. Glasses clinked. Wine flowed like water. And no one really cared about Claire's outburst. "He doesn't own *The Herald.* His family's corporation does. Totally different thing."

"Right. Absolutely. But at least it explains why you're dressed like that."

"Like what?" I scoured the lace bodice of my poppy-colored frock and tugged the tight fabric straight on my hips.

"Like that." She waved her hand in front of me as if performing some witchy magic. "Normally, when you attend a charity event, you remember to bring the back of your dress."

I stood up straighter, letting her snark roll off my half-naked shoulders. "Very funny. I think I look good."

"You do, Holly. Too good. But watch out, looking like that, I might try to take you home with me at the end of the night."

"Wait, what did I just hear? Pajama party at our place?" Austin appeared behind Claire and slipped a flute of champagne into her hand. "It's fine with me. Am I invited?"

"Oh, stop." Claire playfully slapped her hand on his suited chest. He winked then clasped his hand over hers. She sure did a great job cleaning him up for the event. I rarely saw him without a hoodie or ball cap, so his styled blond locks and three-piece suit seemed exceptionally dashing.

"Besides, she's not wearing that outfit for either of us. She has a date."

"I don't have a date. It's a work thing." A sudden tremble shot through my arms and I eyed Claire's drink with immense jealousy.

"It isn't the guy who you stole my gloves for, is it?" Austin added. "Those were some of my favorites."

Claire glared up at him. "Why are you worrying about this? I've never even seen you wear them."

"I might wear them. One day." He shrugged. "But yes, Holly, you look pretty hot tonight." Austin took a sip of his own champagne as Claire nudged him with her elbow in his gut. He coughed and wiped the back of his hand across his mouth.

"Thanks. But it doesn't really matter, anyway. He's

already over a half an hour late so I doubt he's even coming."

Claire grabbed my hand and rubbed her thumb against my knuckles. "I'm sure he's probably just lost or stuck in traffic or something."

"Seriously? Havenbrook is the smallest town in the state and he doesn't have a car here."

She offered me a half-smile, which looked pathetic. I fought the urge to slouch and ruin what was clearly the perfect outfit.

"Or he just wants to make an entrance." Claire nodded her chin over my shoulder, then pointed with her immaculate French manicured finger toward the entrance.

I whirled around on my stilettos to see Ben standing in the lobby craning his neck to scan over the crowded room.

I shrugged and started for the door.

"Go get him," Claire said and tapped my butt as I walked away.

"Alright, Austin, she's cut off."

He ignored me as she settled back against his chest and he kissed the top of her head.

I rushed a few steps then slowed my pace. No reason to hurry. Might as well make an impression. Just like Ben already had. Every head turned to watch the mysterious man near the door. Poised, confident, and oozing enough charm to have every woman in a six-foot radius swooning in seconds. Half the room probably wondered where he came from, and why he'd stumbled into the event. The other half watched him with curiosity, wondering how someone could find a steel blue suit cut so perfect around his broad shoulders in a small town like this. And I just watched, still surprised that he actually showed up to meet me.

Ben swaggered a few steps into the room then stopped dead, his stare glued in my direction, his eyes wide.

"You made it," I asked as I approached. His gaze dropped to the floor for a moment. "I'm so sorry. Meetings ran much longer this afternoon than I had hoped."

"It's fine. I had a bunch of administrative things to help Claire with for the event, anyway. We actually just finished up."

"Good. So, is it fine to say I lied and spent two hours trying to figure out what to wear?"

"Don't you have only about four or five outfits here anyway?"

He laughed, the light returning to his eyes. "Good point. But I thought you said it was only a little fancy?"

He took my hand and leaned forward as his cheek brushed against mine. I froze.

"Because, Holly Brighton," he whispered. "You look far too breathtaking for just a little bit fancy."

He backed away and released my hand.

"I try," I croaked, then cleared my throat, trying to shake the soft touch of his skin. "Now, why don't we head over and get you a drink?"

We maneuvered through the crowd as I tried to

ignore the stares following our every move. He leaned into my ear. "Everyone's looking at you."

"Yeah, I doubt that." His hand rested near the small of my back as we navigated our way, not daring to touch but the heat of his palm scalding the naked skin near my waistline. My little secret as I passed the familiar faces of everyone I'd known since I was a child.

"Well, hello there, Ben." Claire inserted herself between us and the bar, extending her hand in his direction. "It's so nice of you to be able to make it to our little event."

"Not a problem." He took her hand and shook it. "Claire, right? We met at the bar?"

"That's right. However, I didn't realize that I would be seeing you again so soon."

I dropped my head into my hand and wished for the world to open up and swallow me.

"This is my husband, Austin."

Austin shuffled up behind her like a good escort. "Nice to meet you."

She nudged him in the side. "Why don't you run and grab drinks for our friends?"

"It's fine, Claire," I said. "I was just taking Ben over to the bar myself. Thanks though."

"Don't worry about it, it's fine." Austin nodded, his impeccably styled hair starting to come undone as a small piece flipped down onto his forehead before he disappeared into the throng.

The second he was gone, Claire edged up beside Ben and hooked her arm with his. "So, Ben, Holly really hasn't told me too much about you. How long do you expect to be in town?"

He glanced up at me and froze. "I don't know yet. Things are still kind of up in the air."

"Well, Havenbrook really does a great job with Christmas. If you aren't in any hurry, maybe you could hang around through the holidays. Unless you have somewhere to be? Family, girlfriend, whatever?"

Seriously, Claire. I should've known she'd fall into big sister interrogation mode. But, I guess sometimes blunt had its advantages.

Ben stood straighter and politely made some distance between the two of them without being too obvious to Claire. This guy sure knew how to handle himself. Probably years of training from his family's glamorous events.

"Like I said, not really sure where I'm going to be at." He locked eyes with me. "But I don't have a wife or girlfriend to rush back to if that's what you're wondering."

Claire winked at me and I grimaced.

"Two glasses of champagne, coming up." Austin, thankfully, arrived and thrust over-filled glasses into our hands, then slipped his arm over Claire's shoulder. "What did I miss?"

Ben shuffled closer to me and shoved his free hand in his pocket, his elbow brushing against my arm. I shivered in the swelter of the crowd.

"Not much. I was just going to ask about this gala. What exactly is the charity again?" Ben asked.

"Well—" Claire shuffled out of Austin's grip. "All

the money we raise goes toward the children's wing at the hospital."

Ben nodded and rolled his head back, taking in the chandeliers and ornamental sconces on the wall. "Sounds admirable."

"Absolutely. Years ago they were going to close it down, but instead, they created this charity to pay for the operating expenses. Every year the whole town comes together to keep it running," I added.

"Don't be so modest, Holly."

My breath caught in my throat and my eyes widened, glaring down at Claire. No. I screamed with my mind hoping she would get the hint. She didn't.

"It's really Holly's dad who got all of this going. That first year he went door to door in a snowstorm to collect pledges to keep the lights on for all those sick children. He's really the one who kick-started this whole movement. Now it's a great way to get together before the holidays and for a great cause."

"Really?" Ben nudged me with his shoulder and I crossed my arms over my chest. "Sounds like big hearts run in the family."

"Absolutely. Everyone loved Holly's dad. He was an extraordinarily great man."

I waved my right hand across my neck, signaling for Claire to stop, but she didn't notice. Instead, she raised her glass and held it up to Ben. "To David Brighton, the kindest man Havenbrook has ever known."

"Excuse me?" Ben leaned closer to Claire.

She lifted her glass in the air again. "To Holly's dad, David Brighton."

"To David." Ben clinked his champagne flute with hers and glared over at me. I refused to meet his questioning stare and joined the toast, guzzling back half my drink afterward. The bubbles hit my brain immediately but only made things fuzzier.

"Well, this sounds like a wonderful cause, I'm sure Concorde Publications would love to make a donation. Do you know where I might be able to do that?"

"I'll show you." Austin cut through our little group and turned Ben toward the donor station. He slapped him on his back, then glanced back at Claire. She shrugged.

"He seems great," Claire said as soon as both men disappeared.

I turned on my heel and stared at her.

She jerked her head back. "What?"

"Nothing." I sighed and let my shoulders sink, the straps of my dress dangerously close to sliding off. "I just hadn't told him about my dad yet. Or at least not the part about him being editor of *The Herald* for over a decade. It was before Concorde bought the paper, so I'm sure he's figured out we're related, but not how close."

She slid in beside me and wrapped her arm around my waist as she rested her head on my shoulder. "I'm not sure how he would've figured that out from what I said, but I wasn't trying to make you look bad. I was trying to boost you up."

Scooping my arm around her waist, I gave her an

awkward half-hug. "I know, thanks for trying, but I'm sure I just look like a weirdo now. I should have just told him when he asked about him a few days ago. I just didn't want him to disregard my opinion because I was the editor's daughter. I wanted to save the paper because it deserves to be saved."

"He'll get over it. He seems pretty normal. Charming. Sophisticated. Sexy as all hell. You might have just stumbled upon a winner."

"You forgot to mention that he's also practically my boss."

She pinched my chin and steered my face down to meet her eyes. "Then I think someone needs to tell him that. Because the way that man is looking at you is definitely not suitable for work."

"Yeah, right."

She crooked her eyebrow then drained the rest of her champagne. "I'm not blind, Holly." She took my hand and raised it above my head forcing me into a twirl. "And neither is he."

It shouldn't matter. It couldn't matter. But her words swam through my limbs and made them twitch. There were so many reasons why he and I were a bad idea, but why did I not seem to care?

Across the room, Ben stood talking to Jenkins. When did he get here? Must've been in those late meetings too. I took a deep breath and shook out all the weird vibes building up in my blood. All those things I shouldn't feel, but couldn't help myself.

"Well, maybe you should have thought of that sooner," Jenkins muttered as I approached.

"Hello there, Peter. I didn't see you come in. Is Isabelle here as well?" I joined the conversation with a smile making sure not to stand too close to Ben but aching not to be too far from him either.

Jenkins plastered on a smile, but the expression stopped at his lips and didn't quite match the harsh deep-set lines puckered around his eyes. "Why, Holly, don't you look lovely. Yes, Isabelle is around here somewhere. Probably talking to our neighbors again."

Ben watched Jenkins with an icy glare, except he seemed to be more collected than Peter.

"I hope I wasn't interrupting anything?" I backed up a step. "Maybe I should go find her."

"No need. I think we've said all we need to say." Ben cleared his throat and shook off his harsh expression, replacing it with a polite grin.

Jenkins' stare flit between him, then me, and back again. I leaned away from Ben, trying to put as much space between us as possible. Whatever it was, I'd never seen Jenkins this angry, at least not outside of the office. Both men held each other in silent gridlock until eventually Jenkins scoffed and conceded.

"Enjoy the rest of your evening, Holly." Jenkins marched away and disappeared into the crowd.

Ben's shoulders dropped as the tension dissipated.

"What was that all about?" I asked.

"It's nothing." He sounded calm, but couldn't meet my eyes.

Putting my hands on my hips, I tapped my foot. "Peter Jenkins doesn't just give people the death stare. Especially not in public. What's going on?"

He leaned closer, the smell of his expensive cologne clouding my head. "Is there somewhere we can go? To talk."

I pointed at the balcony surrounding the event hall and rushed toward the hidden stairs leading to the upper level. He followed close behind, keeping each step in time with mine. My heels sunk into the plush carpet and I gripped tight onto the banister to keep myself from falling. The thoughts bouncing through my head weren't helping my concentration, nor was the thought of being up here alone with him.

As we crested the top stair, the din of the gala muted into a blur of incomprehensible sounds. The lights faded, leaving both of us draped in shadow, save a few slivers from the chandelier that cut across the angles of Ben's perfect face.

"Why didn't you tell me that David Brighton was your father?"

I crossed my arms and walked silently over to the balcony, watching the people below us swirl about. Colors and sounds, mixing and melding together, but nothing giving me any more clarity.

"Because I didn't want you to know. *The Herald* has always been a huge part of my life. I grew up in that office. I sat on his knee as he edited. I played pretend under the desks when the regular staff went home for the night or on weekends when the edition wasn't as perfect as he'd wanted it to be. It really is my home."

Heat prickled my back as the soft cashmere of Ben's jacket brushed over my skin. His hand appeared next to my waist on the railing as his breath tickled the small hairs on the back of my neck. I shivered and sunk deeper into him. Expensive notes of bergamot folded over the distinct clean smell of the cucumber mint soap from the Starlight. I closed my eyes and inhaled.

"Why did you think I wouldn't understand that? I grew up in a boardroom. Hockey games and soccer practices were cut short by conference calls and last-minute trips. Both my parents worked hard for what they wanted and they built something amazing. It sounds like your dad was just like them."

"Maybe. But I didn't want it to seem like a weakness. You flew into town for business and I'd have hated if you thought I was only doing this for my father. I'm not."

"I know that." His hand moved from the railing and clutched my hip, then he spun me around until we stood face to face. "You have a heart bigger than this whole town, Holly. Maybe this whole state. I wouldn't expect anything less from you."

He lowered his head and the tip of his nose ran down the bridge of mine. Skin on skin. Slow and electric. My hands splayed across his chest as he tugged me tighter, his fingertips lighting sparks like cherry bomb fireworks up my spine.

"I never expected to meet someone like you," he breathed against my cheeks.

"Maybe I should've started kissing random strangers years ago."

He pulled his head back and gazed down at me. His copper eyes appeared endless as if they actually pierced into his soul and let everything pour out. "I'm glad you didn't."

I pushed up onto my toes and let my lips brush against his. Asking. Waiting.

He released his grip on my waist and jerked away. I sunk down onto my heels, wishing I could fall even further through the floor.

My mouth dried as the sting of rejection shot through my limbs, my knees threatening to give way. "I'm sorry. I just thought..."

"Please don't apologize." He let out a long sigh. "I just need to tell you something first."

Pulling back, I leaned against the railing as his face scrunched while he battled whatever he needed to say.

"Remember how you said you would consider taking a reporting job if it came up."

"Yeah, but there isn't one here."

"No, but Peter let me have one of your articles and I sent it to my friend Marcel at the Boston Trumpeter."

I shot up straight, nearly tripping in my heels. "You what?"

"I know I should've asked first, but the good news is that he loved it and wants to offer you a job."

"You had no right to do that." Ice formed in my veins as my stomach hollowed. I clenched my hands into fists. "Is that why Peter was so mad at you? Did you tell him that you were poaching his staff? Please don't tell me he knew about this before I did?"

"Of course not. I wouldn't betray you like that."

"But you would share my work with another editor without my permission and ask them to hire me."

"I didn't ask him. I just sent it along and told him to keep you in mind, but he had a job opening and he loved your work. You should be happy."

I stuck my finger in his face. "Do not tell me how to feel."

"Then don't take the job." He held his hands up in surrender. Except even though he backed down, I still didn't feel any better.

I gripped my arms, suddenly exposed. Nearly naked and humiliated.

"Why couldn't you have just asked me first? Do I really mean that little that I can't have an opinion on my own life?" Who did he think he was? Did being a Concorde suddenly make him the king of all things? Not to me. And I actually trusted him. I was so stupid.

"No, Holly." He stepped forward with his arms open, trying to touch me, but I pulled away. "There just wasn't enough time. I needed to do this now."

"Right. It's almost the holidays and most people are taking vacation. There really isn't any rush."

Ben rubbed his forehead and placed his other hand on his back. His suit jacket rode up as he paced in front of me. "Yes, there is. Remember I told you that *The Herald* needed more ad revenue. Well, we looked at the books again. They need one hundred thousand dollars just to make it until next quarter and nearly five times that to survive for the upcoming year."

"Which means?"

"We're closing *The Herald*. The holiday edition will be its last run. I'd planned on announcing it tomorrow at the morning staff meeting. That's why Peter was so angry, and that's why I rushed out to try to find you that job. After tomorrow you won't have one."

I couldn't breathe. Each word pressed on my ribcage and closed in around my lungs. Heavy. Cement bricks weighing me down. A few tears broke past my lashes and I wiped them off. Mascara streaks painted across my hand, but I didn't care. Nothing mattered right now.

"Why didn't you tell me?"

"I planned on it. I really did, but then I walked in the door and I saw you. So excited to see me and so absolutely gorgeous. All the things I wanted to say didn't matter because I just wanted a few more minutes, or hours, or whatever we had left, seeing you happy. To just be with you."

His compliments died at my feet as I seethed. "Then what? We drink, we dance, you walk me home, and then 'oops, I forgot to mention I'm closing down your entire life in the morning'. Erasing my father's legacy."

He stopped pacing. "To be fair, you didn't tell me about that. At least I planned on telling you about all this. And I really did try to help you out by sending off your article. I wanted to keep you from the fallout."

All this time, I'd fought to keep the paper running. To keep everyone's jobs. My job. But none of it mattered. And how long had he known? Was he plotting all this while we skated in the market? Or maybe while we stood under the stars and he told me how beautiful I was? Did it mean anything or was it just a way to placate me while he razed my whole career to the ground? Except it meant something to me. And he just broke that something then crushed it under the heel of his expensive designer shoes.

"I don't need you to swoop in and save me. I can handle things myself," I said.

"I know you can. But I was looking out for you. Why can't you just let someone care about you?"

"Why? Everyone who cares about me just sets me up and then leaves. Hell, this time I knew you were leaving and still managed to walk into this with both feet."

My hands gripped the banister, hanging on to keep me stable as the room spun around me. Everything crashed and shattered in one moment. The paper. My job. Even my heart. Although Ben, clearly, didn't deserve it in the first place. I hadn't even realized how hard I'd fallen for him until the thought of him leaving cut deep instead of being a relief.

"I hoped we could work that out, but you knew that one day I'd have to go," he pleaded.

I pointed toward the stairs, tears streaming hard down my cheeks and I didn't care to stop them. "Then why don't you get a head start."

He dropped his head to his chest but didn't argue. Each plodding step took his lying mouth further away from me. So, why didn't it feel like a win?

The cold, blustery wind followed me from the cab to the door, nearly pushing me inside. Strains of Christmas music whined from the jukebox, but I didn't have the energy to stumble over to that side of the room to make it stop. Instead, I clicked my stilet-toed feet up to the bar and swung myself around on a stool.

I flopped my arms on the bar top without removing my jacket and stared at the lines of brightly colored liquor bottles along the far counter. Lights glowed from beneath them, adding to the show, and making the thought of a drink all that more enticing.

"You look like you've had a rough night." Danny rested his hands along the bar rail and leaned over me. The soft hint of concern helped ease the strain in my muscles from clenching tight since I raced from the ballroom balcony.

A rough night? To be honest, I wasn't sure. I got my dream job, but I lost the paper. My father's paper. This town's paper. No matter what I might have gained, I'd still lost and let everyone down. If *The Herald* had been suffering so badly, why didn't Jenkins tell anyone? Did he even know? That man worked as hard as any editor in any city, but maybe the finances weren't really his forte. Or was shuttering the paper really the Concorde plan all along? I trembled. Ben could have been lying to me this entire time. Lying to us all.

He didn't seem like he could do something like

that, but how much did I really know him? He'd only been here for a couple of days. One knee-weakening kiss and a few conversations didn't make him innocent. Plus, imagining him as the villain made it so much easier to erase the image of him descending those stairs, broken and defeated. If only there were a way to keep us from being on opposite sides of this?

"Hello, earth to Holly." Danny waved his hand in front of my face. "Can I get you anything?"

I snapped out of my thoughts and looked around. I wasn't used to the place being so quiet. Granted the fundraiser was on tonight, but Danny's Pub was always packed. Successful. An idea started rolling around in my brain. I pushed it down at first, but it roared back, begging to be fleshed out.

"Maybe," I said, drumming my fingers along the wooden bar top. "Have you ever considered advertising?"

CHAPTER ELEVEN

lright, Holly. Deep breaths. I closed my eyes and breathed in slowly, trying to calm my racing heart. The plan backfired, as my jaw thrust open in a deep, almost painful, yawn. I'd barely slept a wink last night, and for the few hours I may have, I tossed and turned more than an ocean in a hurricane. Plus, getting started at 5 AM didn't help matters.

I ran the rest of the way and yanked open the front door of the newspaper office. Doris looked up with her courteous smile quickly morphing into a concerned frown.

"Holly, the meeting has already started. You're late."

"I know," I said as I raced across the lobby. "But there was something I needed to finish. Trust me, it was worth it."

Or at least I hoped it would be.

I chucked my coat and my laptop bag in my cubicle as I rushed toward the board room. Before I reached the windows, I slowed to a relaxed walk, straightening my barely worn suit jacket and pushing my shoulders back. I expected at least a few sets of eyes to notice me, but everyone seemed locked on Ben as he leaned against the head of the table, leading the charge. Wide-eyed expressions and frowning wrinkled mouths hung on his every word. If there was any doubt that he hadn't made the announcement yet, Jenkins' glassy broken stare proved otherwise.

I clutched tighter onto the file folder in my left hand. Only one chance to get this right. Rapping my knuckles on the door, I pushed it open without waiting for an invitation.

Ben halted mid-sentence and glanced up at me. "Thank you for joining us, Ms. Brighton. Now if you could please take a seat so we could continue."

His words came out firm and calm, businesslike to a fault, but his face gave his emotions away. The awkward curl of his bottom lip. The pained glint in his eyes. He'd probably hoped I wouldn't show this morning. Probably would've made this announcement so much easier. But I wouldn't let closing *The Herald* be easy on anyone.

"Thank you, Mr. Concorde, but I think I'd prefer to stand."

He shifted his weight from foot to foot but didn't argue. Instead, he crossed his arms and paced the front of the room, refusing to look in my direction.

"As I was saying, I know that this isn't exactly the news anyone wants to hear, especially before the holidays, but we—" Ben nodded toward Jenkins for support, "—don't have any other options. Effective December 24—"

"I do," I said, raising my hand then feeling silly and dropping it to my side.

"Excuse me?" Ben shook his head and blinked. "You what?"

"I have another option. A few of them, in fact."

I spread the manila file folder open on the board room table and plucked a contract from the top.

"You said we needed to generate more ad revenue, is that correct?"

Ben stood up straighter and crossed his arms. "Of course, but I don't see how—"

"Then here is an order for $60,000 of ad space between now and March."

"That's great, Ms. Brighton, but it's not nearly enough to cover the paper's needs."

"Oh, I know." I grabbed a stack of contracts held together by an overextended binder clip. "That's just the first one. I have over $250,000 of advertising in my hands."

"But—"

"And I know that's just a start. This here—" I pulled the rest of the pages from the file folder, "—is a list of local business owners willing to provide angel investments to keep *The Herald* running."

Jenkins bounded across the room in two quick strides then plucked the list from my hands. He quickly scanned the pages as his eyes widened.

"It all looks pretty legitimate here, Ben." A wary

smile whispered across his mouth, but he pushed it back down.

"Oh, it is. Communities like Havenbrook take care of each other. They trust each other's judgment." I dropped the stack of contracts back on the table with a thud and stared back at Ben. "When everyone heard we needed help, they jumped to offer. They believe in what we're doing here. What this paper means to the people who live in this town."

"So, does this mean we get another chance?" Jenkins gazed between me and Ben. Each of us in the triad of information refusing to make any quick moves. Ben strode toward the exterior window and pressed his fingers along the sill. His knuckles blanched white from the pressure. White as the fluffy flakes of snow falling just outside. He let out a deep controlled sigh, then turned and placed his hand across his forehead.

"Can you all please excuse Ms. Brighton and myself for a few moments? I need to review this new information before making any further comment."

Voices rumbled around us. Concern bordering on hope. Hope I'd given them.

Ben raised his hand toward the door and nodded. As I collected my paperwork, a hot surge rushed through me. Like getting sent to the principal's office for the best senior prank in history. Except I'd never been one to get myself in trouble before. Head held high, I marched toward the door as the dread of confrontation started to claw its way in. Jesse flashed me a thumbs up and a wink as I passed, helping my steps stay light and pushing me forward.

"We can take Peter's office." Ben's voice commanded behind me. I didn't turn around to see his angry expression. I could hear it. Picture the distortion of the face as he realized I'd destroyed his plans. He probably regretted meeting me now.

I hurried into the small office as the door shut hard behind me. Not quite a slam, but enough to make Jenkins' wall of framed diplomas rattle against the eggshell-painted wall.

"What exactly was that in there?" Ben pointed toward the closed door as red seeped up his neck into his defined cheeks.

I crossed my arms and backed up until I leaned against the far bookshelf in the corner. "I just found a way to save *The Herald*, that's all. Doing the work you refused to do."

"And you didn't think to tell me before you stormed into my meeting and made me look like an idiot in front of everyone?"

"Just like you consulted me before sending my private work to a stranger to apply for a job I never asked for?"

He dropped his chin into his chest and grabbed the back of his head. "I said I was sorry about that. I was just trying to help you."

"And I was just trying to help *The Herald*."

"Except this isn't the way it works, Holly. This is a business, not a charity pet project. The advertising revenue is great, but what happens when the investors' pockets are empty or they get tired of supporting a losing cause?"

"Well, at least we will have a chance to turn it around first. You wrote the paper off before they had the opportunity." And us.

"If you'd just told me your plan, I could have helped you. It might not have worked, but you didn't need to shut me out."

Ben quieted and circled around the office running his index finger around the edge of Jenkins' desk until he flopped down in his chair. "When I met you, I was mesmerized by your passion, your heart. The way you care so deeply about things, but I'm starting to think that maybe you're just stubborn. Holding on too tight to things and never letting them breathe. It's exhausting to watch you throw away so much potential that I doubt you even know you have."

I pushed off from the bookcase and walked toward the opposite side of the desk. "What's that supposed to mean?"

"If I need to explain, then you clearly don't get it. The paper, your ex, this whole town, it's just you could do so much...and we could..." His stare dropped to his hands knotted in his lap. "Never mind. Obviously, everything I've done since I got here was a mistake. You can dismiss everyone from the boardroom while I sort through this mess you left for me."

I stood in silence for a moment, but he never

looked up. Eventually, I placed the file folder on the desk in front of him, my hand pausing on the papers for much longer than necessary. I'd walked in here this morning with one mission in mind, but now it didn't feel quite as victorious. The tightness growing in my chest hurt more than it should.

"Ben, I…" Except there was nothing more to say. At least not right now.

My hand lingered on the doorknob but eventually made the move to turn it. "This probably means nothing, but if we were on the same side maybe things would've been different."

"Except that you couldn't see that we always were." He finally looked up. I expected anger, but only pain shone through his eyes. "I get that Havenbrook and *The Herald* are your anchors, but if you don't let go, you're just going to drown."

"Maybe, but at least I have something I'd be willing to risk my life for."

The hollow thunk of the door closing between us echoed through the office. Ben on one side and me on the other. It was probably for the best.

CHAPTER TWELVE

*S*tubborn? Who was Ben to call me stubborn? Mr. I'm-all-corporate-stooge-all-the-time telling me I need to relax. I wrote the word down in thick block letters on my notepad and traced them over and over again until the pen tip cut through the page. Clearly, I'd moved on to another stage of processing our argument in Jenkins' office. Already lunchtime and he still hadn't emerged. The door remained closed tight. Even Jenkins sat in an empty bullpen desk to avoid disturbing him.

An unusual silence fell over the office. Whispers and hushed tête-à-tête's wafted around, but no one seemed to dare to speak aloud.

I'd tried to write several times, but the words just wouldn't come. Most of them were tied up in my head, piecing together all the things I should have said when I had the chance. When I could have told Ben what I was really thinking. Except I still hadn't sorted that out yet. I scrolled mindlessly through my email.

So many "Ask Holly" questions punctuated with the desperate junk mail pleas of stores trying to get those last-minute sales less than a week before Christmas. My computer dinged as another email arrived.

MDupre@BostonTrumpeter.com
Job Offer

I hovered my mouse over the hyperlink as my fingers twitched. It wouldn't hurt to just look at the message. Obviously, I wasn't going to take it, but it didn't mean I couldn't find out what the market looked like for my level of experience. To be honest, it would almost be irresponsible of me not to read it. I clicked the mouse button.

Ms. Brighton,

I received your information from Benjamin Concorde, and...

I hit delete without reading any further. No point. Just seeing his name sliced deep into my heart. Scars that I should get started on healing.

After slamming my laptop shut, I wrestled my phone from my purse.

Me: *Coffee?*

Three little dots appeared immediately.

Claire: Sure. Meet you at Corner Brew in 10.

A hit of roasting espresso blasted my face as I pushed open the door. Instead of jumpstarting my pulse, today it had the opposite effect. Claire waved from her favorite table by the window as she sat, her chin propped up on her hand, watching the town go by.

I popped up on the bar height chair and flipped open the plastic lid on the coffee cup already sitting in my place.

"I guessed it was a double shot mocha kind of day." Claire shrugged and scanned my face looking for clues. "So, what is going on with you? I saw you rush out of the gala last night and then you don't answer any of my calls or texts. What happened?"

I took a long sip and let the chocolatey goodness roll down my tight throat. My shoulders sank, a slight pain prickling through the muscles I'd held taut for the whole morning.

"No, it wasn't you. It was that Ben guy I invited. Big mistake," I said.

"Really? I kind of liked him. He seemed kinda nice."

"Yeah, a nice guy that was about to close down *The Herald* for good."

Claire slammed her palm on the table and it echoed through the small café. The barista behind the counter glared at us.

"You're kidding? And you're just saving that piece

of gossip until now. Why didn't you tell me yesterday?" Claire asked.

"Because I had to do something. I couldn't just sit back and let this happen, so I spent all night calling and visiting half of Havenbrook to get the money we needed to stay open."

"Wow. You're kind of amazing, you know that?" She winked at me and took another sip of her Chai latte. "But why didn't you ask me for help?"

"Because apparently, I'm selfish and stubborn." I took a giant gulp of my coffee and let the burn sting all the way down.

"Says who?" Her face soured as she sat up straight in her chair. If anyone would throw down for me, it was Claire. It's a good thing I didn't call her back yesterday, she might have hunted Ben down.

"Ben." I dropped my head and picked at the adhesive order label on my cup. The cutesy little hearts and snowflakes drawn on the side didn't even lighten the heaviness bearing down on my ribs. "I might've, kind of, thrown my entire save *The Herald* plan at him during a well-attended staff meeting."

Claire sucked air through her teeth as her face mimicked how awful I felt. "Yikes. Not a great move, but everyone should still be pleased with what you've done. Besides, that wasn't any reason to call you selfish. Saving *The Herald* is a pretty selfless act, or at least I think so."

"Okay, maybe he didn't exactly call me selfish, but definitely stubborn. Those words 100% came out of his mouth."

"Why do I feel like there's more to this than you're telling me?"

"Not really." I set my elbows on the tabletop and held my head in my hands trying to make the thoughts stop. "Only that Ben submitted my writing to an editor in Boston and they offered me a reporting job."

Claire's expression perked up. "Holly, that's fantastic."

"But I'm not taking it."

She leaned back on her chair. Her nose scrunched up like it always did when she needed to pick her words carefully. "And why, exactly? You've been talking about a reporter job forever."

"Yeah, but not like this. I'm not just going to up and leave everything I know for that."

"No wonder he called you stubborn."

I crossed my arms and scoffed at her insult. "Wow, that's fair."

"Seriously, you've been going on and on about how you wanted this job and you haven't gotten it. Heck, the night you met Ben you'd gone off on one of your rants about how you were going to look elsewhere if Peter didn't give you what you wanted, now all of a sudden you're doubling down on staying here in Havenbrook? I'd be pretty confused too if it weren't for the fact that I knew you were all talk about leaving."

I pushed up from my chair and snatched the cup off the table. "So, you've just been humoring me this whole time? Nice."

"Sit back down, drama queen. I have supported you through everything, and I knew you'd finally leave when you were ready. Everything you've been through has held you back here, but other than me, what is really holding you back now?" She shook her head as if I might answer, but I stayed silent. "One of the things I love most about you is how you dream so much bigger than the rest of us, but it breaks my heart to see that most of the time they're just dreams. You got out of here once and I was so, so proud of you and I get why you needed to be here for your dad. But then you met Fletcher, and he just held you back and I hoped that, finally, now that you'd ended things you'd be able to move on, but you're still just as stuck."

I stood still, one foot facing the door but refusing to move. Her words washed through me filtering through many levels of my heart. Anger filtered into irritation into sadness, into something that might have resembled acceptance, but I wasn't sure yet.

Claire placed her hand on mine and gripped my fingers. "You are my best friend in the whole world, and that is never going to change, but you have to stop letting good things pass you by because the last time you left things didn't work out how you planned. I'm telling you this, because I care about you, and because I know you'd tell me if I needed to hear the same. But don't lose out on your future because you can't let go of the past."

Was she right? Was I sabotaging my entire life to hang on to my dad and this town? My mind raced, picking apart every decision I'd made over the past few years. Every little choice I made kept me here, but is this really where I wanted to be or because I felt I needed to? Maybe. Maybe not. Everything blurred. Claire's words mixed with Ben's that mixed with all my messy emotions in one big cocktail that I needed to swallow. And even though things hadn't become completely clear, my heart knew I'd made a huge mistake.

"Holls, say something to me." She tugged at my hand as she cast me a teary gaze.

"I..." I grabbed my coffee and chugged back the rest of the cup. Words jumbled in my head. So many things to say. So many apologies to make. I grabbed her hand and tugged her close, burying my face in her shoulder. "I love you the most, you know that, right? I'm really sorry."

She squeezed me back. "It's okay. I know I'll pay you back with a crisis sooner or later. I always do."

After letting go, I rubbed my hands over my face and tried to collect myself the best I could. "There's something I've got to do. I'll call you later, okay?"

"Go make things right, Holly," Claire said, as she waved me toward the door.

Bursting out onto the busy sidewalk, my feet ran faster than my brain could catch up. He had no right to call me out, but clearly Ben saw what everyone else did, and that I somehow couldn't. It didn't make things better, but I needed to talk to him. Needed to hear more. Needed to apologize.

"Afternoon Doris," I called as I raced through the lobby.

"Holly, wait."

I skidded to a halt.

"Didn't you get the message? Peter has just recalled everyone to the boardroom. Hurry up, dear."

I bounded through the empty office and whipped out my phone. Yep, eight missed messages from Jesse, two from Jenkins, and fifteen from Doris. Shoving the phone back in my pocket, I crept into the boardroom.

"Just in time," Jenkins said from the head of the table. "I'm happy to announce that due to Holly's hard work and ingenuity, *The Herald* will remain open."

Cheers erupted around the table and Jesse patted me on the shoulder.

"Good work, 'Ask Holly'," he said.

Jenkins raised his open hand in the air and the voices stopped. "This doesn't mean we don't have a lot of work to do. This experience should teach us all how important it is to make sure we are taking care of our business, as well as doing the best job that we can. We owe this community more than ever now. So, let's go forth and make this the best holiday edition of *The Herald* that they've ever seen. A giant thank you card to Havenbrook."

Everyone rose and headed for the door. I looked around again, however the likelihood that I missed him in the small room seemed impossible. "Peter," I whispered across the table. "Where's Ben? ... I mean Mr. Concorde."

Jenkins smirked. "He already left. Said there wasn't anything more he could do here."

My feet tapped below the table. I'd missed him. I wasn't even gone that long.

"Okay." I jumped up and weaseled my way into the main office then zig-zagged through the cubicles to get back out the door.

"Where are you going now?" Doris called after me.

"To fix things," I yelled back, even though I had no clue how.

I dashed through the snowy streets, the sun reflecting off the white banks and nearly blinding me without my sunglasses. But I knew this town better than anyone, even if I couldn't see, I could still find my way.

In the distance, the neon Starlight sign glowed dim in the daylight. My stomach twisted and turned, my typical regret trying to eat its way into my bloodstream, but I wouldn't let it. I didn't have time.

I slowed near the lobby and struggled to catch my breath, as I pushed the door open in front of me. I speed walked my way to the left passing the main check-in counter, my head down on a mission.

"He's not there, Holly."

I wrenched my head back. Robbie stood behind the counter with his hands on his hips.

"What?" I said.

His wide sympathetic stare weighed down on my shoulders. "You just missed him by about twenty minutes. Some fancy car service came by and collected him."

"How did you know that's—"

"Don't try to pull one over on me. I see all sorts of

people every single day and there is no way that the devastated look on his face when he left could match the one on yours right now without there being a story behind it."

I tripped forward and slammed my hand against the wall as the world began to spin.

"Are you okay?" Robbie rushed from his post to pour me a glass of lemon water from the public dispenser.

The swirl of emotions finally caught up with my feet and ricocheted through me. I was too late. All the things Claire said about giving up on what I wanted and the only thing I knew for a solid fact seemed to be that Ben was one of those precious things. I'd messed up. I'd made an idiot of myself. And who knew if I would ever get a chance to make it right.

CHAPTER THIRTEEN

"*I*t's going to be strange without your smiling face around here, sweetie." Jesse blinked as he rolled his wet eyes up toward the ceiling.

I wrapped my arms around him and inhaled, trying to lock more memories into my brain for a rainy day. I'd have to grow into a city like Boston and lonely days would definitely be on the horizon. "I'll miss you too. Give me a call if you are ever up that way."

"Of course. And remember to have a Merry Christmas."

He flashed me a kind smile and rushed out the front door toward the street. My shoulders sank. I thought I'd have more time after I accepted Marcel's job offer, but he wanted me by the new year and I'd already written enough columns to last that long for *The Herald*. With the holidays thrown in the mix, it just made sense to go while I could. Besides, if I waited too long, I'd have too many chances to talk myself out of leaving. Although, Claire would probably shake me senseless if I did.

I shifted back and forth on my feet, scanning the office for something or someone I might have missed, but with it already Christmas Eve, no one really worked much today anyway, so I had the entire day to get myself organized. Only one thing left on my list. The one goodbye I'd been dreading.

Rapping my knuckle against the flimsy door, I peeked inside Jenkins' office. Bottles of scotch with brightly colored bows sat in a perfect line on the side of his desk, but he ignored them, poring over a printed copy of last quarter's financials.

"Do you have a minute?" I asked, opening the door wider and edging into the office.

"Absolutely, Holly. C'mon in." He pulled his reading glasses from his nose and rubbed his eyes. "Just finishing up."

"I won't be long. I just wanted to say goodbye before I left."

I tucked my hands behind my back, suddenly unsure what to do with them as Jenkins stretched out in his chair. A sigh erupted from his lips as his body deflated like a giant man-shaped balloon.

"I guess that's it then?" Jenkins scratched the back of his head and looked toward the floor, as a sheen slid over his gaze. "I know I can't convince you to stay, so I won't try, but thank you so much for all you've done for this paper and for me. These last few weeks have been the most stressful of my life and somehow you managed to make things better. At least for now."

"Of course, Peter. You're the first one who gave me a chance and I love it here, but..."

"You don't need to explain. I get it. You've given me an amazing gift, now it's my turn to make sure I keep things in line and maintain *The Herald* legacy. I owe you that." His throat bobbed as he swallowed, then he extended his hand. "I might have given you your first chance, but your talent is much bigger than Havenbrook. I'm sure we won't hear the last of you, and whatever comes out, we'll all be proud. I know your father, wherever he is, sure will be. He always knew you were destined for greatness."

"Thanks. That means a lot." I took his hand and shook it while his soft wrinkled fingers trembled in my grip. His soft green eyes misted over completely and my throat ached harder with each welling tear. He opened his arms wide and pulled me into a hug. My ribs tightened around my heart as it threatened to burst. "I'll miss you, Peter. Merry Christmas."

"Merry Christmas to you, too. Now go, before I regret not begging you to pass up that fancy city job."

I nodded, my words sticking in my throat like shards of glass. Besides, nothing I could say would be enough. Wiping my hand over my eyes and casting a few stray tears to the carpet, I rushed out of the office.

"Oh, Holly, one last thing."

I froze but refused to turn around.

"Could you answer one last 'Ask Holly' letter

before you go? I think it would be an amazing addition to our holiday edition."

"I've already turned in my laptop and—" I glanced at my phone and tapped the screen, "—it's almost six on Christmas Eve, haven't we closed the issue already?"

"Do an old man a favor and give it a read. I left a copy on your desk. If it's not something you're interested in doing, I'm sure I can find someone else to answer the poor soul."

I peeked back over my shoulder. A strange smile twisted on Jenkins' face as he pulled my strings. Couldn't let me walk away, could he? But one last letter couldn't hurt. Besides, I didn't have anywhere to be. What would I do tonight, anyway? Go home and pack my bags just to sit and wait for the next week to pass before my flight?

Eerie silence settled over the office. The last of the late staff had left, probably off to family dinners or other gatherings. The emptiness hollowed my stomach. This was it. I was finally going. I scurried to my empty desk, the weight of my decision boring down on my shoulders. A folded piece of crisp white paper sat in the middle of my barren desk. I eyed the letter and shook my head. No. Why drag this out and make it harder to leave? I needed to be done.

While shrugging into my jacket, I scooped up my purse and unclipped my office pass card then rested it on the desk next to the crystal snowflake I didn't need to bring with me. I sighed. A new beginning. Shouldn't this be easier? Or maybe it wasn't that I didn't want to move on, but that I'd hoped a certain someone would have waited around to see me off. But that would be too much to ask for someone like him.

I marched through the office for the last time, slowly taking every detail in. The cluttered maze of the bullpens. The earthy smell of printer ink. My home for so many years, except now it wasn't, and for the first time since I'd finally made the decision to go, it didn't seem so scary anymore.

Red and green lights from the street reflected across the shiny reception floor. Another Christmas in Havenbrook. Possibly my last, who really knew? A strange calm settled over my body. But whatever happened, I was going to be okay. My hand hovered over the doorknob heading out into the snowy twilight. Maybe I should answer just one last Christmas wish.

Ripping off my coat, I stormed back through the office, grabbing a pad of paper and a pen in my fury. Just fifteen minutes. That's it. I'd put together an answer and the team could edit it to polish later. I settled into my chair and clutched the letter in my hands. Even if I couldn't have everything I wanted this holiday, it didn't mean that I couldn't help someone else have theirs.

Dear Holly,

I met the most amazing woman. Intelligent, charming, and the biggest challenge I've ever encountered. But I've completely blown my chances with her. She's the advice columnist at The Havenbrook Herald, and I'm starting to think I should have listened to her more. The entire town trusts her opinion, why didn't I? I let my work and my ego affect my judgment and I regret it.

If I stand under the mistletoe in the middle of the skating circle at seven o'clock on Christmas Eve, do you think she'll show up so I can tell her how I feel? If she doesn't, maybe I already have my answer.

Sincerely,
Needing Just One More Chance

CHAPTER FOURTEEN

*T*he festive lights of Havenbrook glinted and glittered along the snowy sidewalk, casting a celestial glow against the empty streets and darkened shop windows. The whole town had already closed down for the holidays. Except for me, as my boots slipped and slid on the ice in my frenzied rush toward the Christmas market. At least if I fell, no one would be around to see me land on my butt.

As I rounded the final corner, I wrestled my phone from my pocket and slowed to a walk. 6:58. Right on time. If I hadn't sat at my desk reading Ben's letter and letting my thoughts play out all the different things I could say, all the ways this could go, I wouldn't have had to run. I also wouldn't be gasping like a weirdo trying to calm my heavy awkward breaths before I made my way to the end of the market. And even worse, I still didn't have a clue what to say.

Bright white snowflakes glowed against the backdrop of city hall and the soft chords of a soulful jazz *Jingle Bells* echoed off the brick buildings from the skating pond, beckoning me closer. Drawing me in. Ahead, the shiny surface of the ice glimmered in the moonlight, casting shadows around a figure standing stoic in the center. My face warmed. Like the hot July sun kissing my cheeks amidst the December frost. He was really here. I wrapped my arms around my chest, clutching my coat closer to my body, and picked up my pace.

I reached the edge of the skating circle and eased my toe out onto the slick surface, as a strange weightless sensation flowed through my limbs.

"Hey," I called out as I slipped my way across the pond.

Ben's head rose from his chest and a flicker of hope lit in his eyes. "You came."

"Yeah. I received an 'Ask Holly' letter asking for help, and at *The Herald*, we take our advice column very seriously."

He nodded. "Well, in that case, I have a huge problem."

"Oh, yeah?" I narrowed my stare and thrust my hands to my hips, as I finally closed the gap between us. "Tell me all about it."

His lip twitched as if he might smile, but it faded as quickly as it appeared. He hung his head again. "There's this woman. She's smart, strong, and stubborn as hell, and I just can't seem to get her out of my head."

"So," I nodded and tapped my finger across my lips, "what exactly is the problem?"

"I hurt her. I shouldn't have, but I did, and now I'm supposed to be on a plane halfway across the country, but I couldn't bring myself to board. I regret how I treated her when she was only trying to help. If I'd just listened to what she'd been trying to tell me the whole time, maybe I wouldn't have made such a huge mistake." He lifted his head and pinned me with his stare. Wide-eyed and open. Fragile. Like whatever I said could save him or shatter him into a million unfixable pieces. "What do you think I should do to get her to forgive me?"

I studied his face. The hard cut of his jaw that I ached to rest my hand against and let it melt into my palm. His deep, dark lips I dreamed of kissing again since the night we met.

"First of all, I'd apologize and make sure I told her everything you've just told me. I'm sure she's been waiting to hear it," I said.

"Holly, I am so—"

I raised my hand and rested it on his chest. "I wasn't finished. I'd also make sure that she apologized for her own behavior. I shouldn't have made such a scene in front of everyone. When I knew about the sponsors I should have tried to talk to you in private or at least given you a heads up. I was angry and frustrated and I made a bad decision."

"Maybe, but it's your decision that rescued *The Herald*. You asked me to help save the paper and that's not what I did. It wasn't on purpose, I just followed the regular Concorde business model and didn't open my mind to the other possibilities. Sometimes community support is bigger than facts and figures. I only tried using my head, you used your heart as well."

"Well, now you have a second chance with them too." I tugged at the collar of his jacket. "I've only bought the paper a few years to turn things around and they're going to need someone to help them through it. Unfortunately, I won't be here to do it."

He nodded. "I heard. Marcel told me you took the job in Boston. What changed your mind?"

"You did...with a little help from Claire, of course. You were right about me. Havenbrook is my home, but my future isn't here. Just my past. I thought I needed *The Herald* because it kept me closer to my father, but I think I'm a lot more like him than I originally thought." I glanced out toward the newspaper exhibit near city hall. I didn't need to see his picture; it was already locked in my memory. Forever. "He'll always be with me, even if I'm not here. It's time to start my own life and make my own dreams come true."

"I'm really happy for you. I think you are going to love it there and Marcel is amazing. But, I won't be the one handling Havenbrook anymore."

"What?" My hand jerked, but he rested his gloved fingers over mine, keeping me from yanking it away.

"The thought of getting on another plane and leaving everything behind again made me sick to my stomach. I called my parents and told them I needed to start living my life, one that is more than offices and hotel rooms."

I gasped and squeezed his hand. "You quit your own company?"

"No, of course not." He laughed. "But we're going to make some changes. Starting with distributing some of my responsibilities to others in the organization. Then I'll have my pick of any home office under the Concorde umbrella."

"That's amazing, Ben." I smiled, but my throat clenched. Both of us seemed to be getting exactly what we wanted, so why did it feel like a loss? "Where are you going to choose?"

"Anywhere I want. There's a new office opening in San Francisco that could use my help. Or—" His voice lowered. The tone shaky, for once, uncertain. "There's a struggling publication just outside of Boston. I think I could do a lot of positive things there if I had a good enough reason to go."

"Wouldn't that make you direct competition for my new employer?"

"Probably. But it would also mean that we'd both be in the same city." He dragged out the final words. A question without actually asking. So much more than a business decision.

The streams of Christmas carols echoed on the breeze, but neither of us made any other sounds. Could he really be serious? Could he honestly want to be with me?

"But I also hear there's a spot for me in Florida. A lot less snowy than the east coast, unless..."

His burnished copper eyes begged me to say yes. To tell him what he wanted to hear. That one little word sat so readily on my tongue, but I bit it back.

"This is an important change for you. I shouldn't be part of your decision, Ben."

"But what if I want you to be?"

And I wanted to be. But after being burned by Fletcher, could I take another blow if he decided he missed his jet-set former life? But Ben wasn't Fletcher. He wasn't anything like any other man I'd ever known.

"Fine, then tell me one thing." He released my hand and backed up a step. I shivered as the cool breeze between us brushed against my skin. "What would you tell one of your readers if they sent you this question?"

I paused. It was so easy. I'd had so many similar questions over the years. "I'd tell them to follow their heart."

"And I know what my heart is telling me, what's yours?" Ben pulled off his glove and pressed his hand against my cheek. I leaned into his touch as all my worries drained and pooled at my feet.

"It's telling me that you'll really love it in Boston."

He smiled; his lips so close. His soft breath fell on my frozen nose, warming me from the outside in.

"I think so too. I'll have them finalize the transfer next week."

"Wait. You already knew I'd say yes?"

"No. I just hoped. But there is one more thing to deal with."

I frowned and glanced around the empty square.

Ben pointed his finger to the sky. I tilted my head up toward the white berries and dark green leaves of mistletoe tied to the string of lights above our heads.

I chuckled and shook my head against his palm. "Are you going to make me kiss you again?"

"I think this time it's my turn. Besides, I've been wanting to kiss you for so long now."

He pressed his full mouth to mine, and I pushed up on my tiptoes to meet him halfway. My hands laced around the back of his neck, as his strong lips massaged away the last of my doubts. I let go, falling deeper into his soft rhythm, the real thing so much better than in the dreams I'd forced myself to forget. Now all my dreams seemed to be coming true and I couldn't wait for the future. But I doubted it would have any moments more perfect than this.

I broke my face away and whispered, "Merry Christmas, Ben."

He smiled and kissed me gently on my forehead. "Merry Christmas, Holly."

ABOUT THE AUTHOR

Born and raised in Northern Manitoba, Scarlett Kol grew up reading books and writing stories about creatures that make you want to sleep with the lights on. She also has a soft spot for romance and adores a good love story.

Connect with Scarlett on social media or on her website www.scarlettkol.com.

facebook.com/scarlettkolauthor
instagram.com/scarlettkol
bookbub.com/profile/scarlett-kol

ALSO BY SCARLETT KOL

Never miss a new release from Scarlett Kol by signing up for her newsletter.

DYSTOPIAN

Mercury Rises

PARANORMAL

Wicked Descent

Keeper of Shadows

Sleepless

FARAWAY HIGH FAIRYTALES

Falling

Dreamer

CPSIA information can be obtained
at www.ICGtesting.com
Printed in the USA
LVHW041158040921
696873LV00008B/536

9 781777 635015